The Truth About Eddie
The Beginning

By Joseph Sexton

DeliBerately diStrEssed GrAmmer

The Truth About Eddie: The Beginning by Joseph Sexton
Copyright © 2019. All rights reserved.

Published by Pen It! Publications, LLC
812-371-4128
www.penitpublications.com

Published in the United States of America by Pen It! Publications, LLC
ISBN: 978-1-950454-38-9

Introduction

If you were to ask anyone in the county about Artie/Eddie, you'd hear something like, "Why sure I know that rascal. He's the supreme trouble-maker, he's the source of all evil, but somehow the law can't see it, and half the town-folk pamper him. He's a pest---he's a worm!" And yet, ninety percent had a sort of twisted love for the guy!

They tell stories about how bad he is, how good he is. A large portion tells about how good he is at being bad. Most all claim to hate him and yet they depend upon him for entertainment that is varied and unexpected to the nth degree. The pranks occur every few months, leaving the town reeling and someone, usually the elderly Doc Thomas, crouching back in a corner; baffled and cross-eyed from trying to figure out what has happened.

Table of Contents

Yarn 1
Healin' Prowler

There was one yarn that everybody knew about, and they'd chewed on it until it could almost be swallowed. It was about a good deed gone wrong. It was both funny and sad. It made some folks laugh and other folks mad. Considering the war between Doc Thomas and a thirty year old juvenile delinquent and his group of camp followers, Doc should have caught on after all the times he'd been the target, but he was slow to learn; having to ponder the least thing next to forever. There were rules to most things in life—he knew that, but when it came to these crazy pranks, well—no one had figured out when a prank would erupt into chaos. Most folks had stopped trying and were just holding their breath; waiting for the next jolt to come.

Doc Thomas owned a veritable passel of hound dogs, and he was right proud of every one of them. Mostly they ran the neighborhood sorting trash the way dogs will, but just as mostly keeping an eye out for lady dogs that were willing to forget about being ladies.

Now Doc; he really weren't a doctor, nor even a veterinarian, but most everyone called him Doc; well, he had this one hound that he was right extra proud of except for one thing. The dog was a car chaser and neither Doc nor anyone else had been able to break him of the habit; not until, that is, Doc happened to mention it to a bunch of fellows sitting around tables in the rear of the general store.

There they sat, swapping lies, and spitting their Beechnut into paper cups and other containers and with Doc present the talk just naturally turned to dogs.

"Can't learn Ol' Prowler a durned thang," he moaned. "He goes around chasing ever' car that comes along. I 'spect it's just a matter of time before someone squishes the innards outta him.

Contrariest dog I reckon I ever seed."

Doc wasn't going to pen the dogs up no matter how big a bother they might be to other folks.

"Dogs are wild critters; 'sposed to be that way---not penned up. If they get squashed, then I reckon they just get squashed."

"Doc," says Artie, "I'd be mighty glad to fix Prowler, and I'd get it done right smartly, too."

"The heck, you say-----you reckon you could?"

"Ain't no doubt about it. They's ways, and then again, they's ways. I'm betting I can learn him right off the bat not to go chasing cars. I'll tell you Doc, when I cure him, he'll tuck his tail and run if he so much as sees ary a thang that's got a wheel on it. He'll run from a wheelbar, or a rollerskate I reckon. Oh, and don't ever drop a marble near him."

"Well," says Doc, getting all glassy eyed. "If'n you can get it done I'd be much obliged."

"Awright," says Artie. "See that he's in front of your house at three o'clock, because that's when I'll be by to heal him."

Neither Doc nor anyone else had any idea in what direction or how far Artie's treatment was likely to go, but Doc figured anything was better than having to scrape Prowler off the blacktop. That hound was probably the valueablest dog in the state.

Three o'clock was a little more than an hour away, so Doc left to make arrangements; no way was he about to be late for Prowler's healing.

Artie waited half an hour, then drove his old '56 Ford pickup to his house, got out and entered the woodshed. When he emerged, he carried a large screwdriver, a hard rubber mallet, and a burlap bag. He squinted at the sun and figured if he drove real slowly, he'd arrive at Doc's place right on time.

It was five minutes short of three when Artie stopped and got out a hundred yards from his target. He walked around to the passenger's side, a smile on his face that rivaled the sun. He was about to operate on a hound dog and his prognosis was the operation would be an unqualified success. He pried the hubcap from the right rear wheel, draped the bag across the hub, and hammered the hubcap into place.

He could see Doc standing in his front yard, at least a dozen dogs around him. It seemed half the men in town had heard the news----Artie was going to do his thing---again, and they were curious to see how he would do it. Even more, they wanted to see what would happen afterward.

As mentioned before, everyone had their own opinion about this prankish kid who was somewhere around his thirtieth year. It was always an experience to witness the workings of a mind such as Artie's----- a guy who must still be smarting from the broom-handle attack directed by his ever-loving wife; but that's another story, a long time gone, and her along with it.

Now all the guys were out of their vehicles, shuffling around, trying to get a good view of----they knew not what. All could see Artie's truck; it was moving slowly, then a little faster. And they could hear the slapping of the burlap, but few knew what it might be. Some crossed the road; figuring that whatever was going to happen would likely occur over there, but before many could move it was all over.

Artie had driven toward Doc's house, and Prowler had streaked across the grass, hit the pavement and made a grab at the awful thing that swirled toward him. He made a poor grab, but it was still too much.

Prowler slapped the pavement a couple of times, then came loose and spun into the air with his neck spiraled around like a corkscrew. He landed in a sitting position, a look of great perplexity on his face, then he up and ran for the house, and dived into the crawl space.

Artie had been right about one thing; the hound was cured of car chasing. In fact, he was so well healed he had to be pried from under the house at feeding time. He no longer chased wheels----wouldn't if they carried the neatest girlie dog in the county---- in the state! In truth, the dog wouldn't hunt anything at all. Of course Doc blamed Artie for ruining his best dog; hated him for it. But Artie wasn't to blame----he said so.

"Don't blame me, Doc," he said, "Blame Prowler!"

Well, everyone went around wearing an air of expectancy; waiting to see what Doc would do in retaliation, and they didn't have long to wait. The old fella got a bag of his own and filled it with walnuts. He'd sit on his porch, surrounded by his hounds, and watch for Artie who had to pass by on the way to his job----or else drive about ten extra miles out of his way. So far, he'd braved the old fellow, and protected himself by putting poultry wire over the passenger side window whenever it was rolled down, which in this hot weather was most of the time.

"Here he comes now," Doc thought. He grabbed a walnut and placed it in his slingshot, and pulled back. He would dearly love to crack an especially hard walnut on Artie's hard head.

Thus far Doc had not thought to use something that would pass through the wire; a marble maybe. But Doc had walnuts aplenty, and was mighty short on marbles; was the opinion of most folks. Now, at just the right instant Doc let fly. A good and true aim it was too. It hit the wire plumb dead center and bounced off.

Under the porch Prowler scrooched back as far as possible, and set up the most pitiful mourning and moaning, and general carrying on at the thought of those dreadful wheels passing no more than a couple of good jumps away. For the next forty eight hours the hound would be lost in a tangle of night-mares and not even a scorched pizza could tempt him out.

During the next few hours Artie did the strangest thing, puzzling his cadre of trouble makers as well as the town's folk. Most figured it was due to some money matters that involved his ex-wife, but that turned out not to be.

Artie---his full name was Edward Arthur Reardon; he had been nick-named, "Ears," when he was a school kid----his peers using all his initials to form a name that would fit.

Well, now he had grown a bit tired of Artie. He considered it too sissified. Besides, as famous as he'd become lately, he was due a name with a more vibrant ring to it; he became 'EDDIE!' He insisted the others refer to him as such, and so it went. Soon it could be heard all around the small city. Wherever busybodies and merchants sat or wandered, the gab now was of Eddie and his shenanigans. Who would have thunk it?

As time often will it slid away, and things settled down, and it became reasonably calm again. People began to wonder where Artie---er, Eddie had gone. It became so quiet around the diners and the 'burger' joints that it seemed an all-together different town. It was easily explained; something or someone was missing, and it didn't take a genius to know who that must be; a person of questionable reputation, and in that part of the world it could be none other than Eddie!

Eddie was seldom seen in the area. The whole gang who had depended on the rascal for their main hours of entertainment was beginning to worry and fret. They sent out scouts to pick up some trace of the thirty year old juvenile. The news wasn't good. They heard of some of his works on the far side of the county, but since most of the guys shied away from steady employment, few of them could afford to drive all over creation and half of Columbia for their entertainment. Consequently they missed out on some really good pranks. Even old Doc

Thomas had put away his sack of walnuts, and was spending much of his time nourishing his anger and wondering at the crazy tricks the county rascal had pulled off over the years.

And then one day Eddie showed up. From time to time he could be seen sauntering along, hands in pockets, pondering sneakier pranks. The idlers around town sat here and there in little groups---talking about the good old days when memories were made that would last a life-time and on into the big darkness and beyond. In time, all of Eddie's disciples gathered in the back of the general store.

All were trying to out-talk the others when the chimes sounded and Doc Thomas, smelling pre-xactly like a dog kennel, walked in. Since there were no more chairs available, he found an empty vegetable crate, up ended it, and sat down. The talk faded just enough for Doc to hear Pete Simpson ask, "you run outta' walnuts, Doc?"

"I can get more," Doc answered sourly, looking around the dimly-lit space for the newly re-named demon, but the rascal wasn't there.

Doc wasn't sure if that fact pleased, or displeased him. There just wasn't any way to judge what Doc cottoned to. He changed from minute to minute if he was feeling normal, but no one had any idea when that might be.

Doc had been studying on the problem for a while and he figured, given time, he'd come up with a way to pay Eddie back for turning his best dog into a clawless little kitten. It'd been a few months now and so far, Doc claimed the pain from that episode hadn't eased a bit, but he could feel a plan shaping up. As soon as he resolved some problems, one of them would be gone, and Doc allowed he wasn't the one who'd be leaving. It would be a heaven-sent gift if Eddie just sorta' faded away never to be seen or heard of again---swallowed by a mosquito or some such. Melted into ooze, maybe.

It was not to be though because wherever folks gathered, stories about Eddie were a prime subject. It seemed there was no end to the tales about the rapscallion who should have been tossed into the county jail where the bars were cold enough to stick his tongue----make it so as all he could say was something like, A—E—EYE---OH—OOOO! That would give decent people a rest until the deputies ran out screaming and pulling at their hair.

And of course, to hear Eddie tell it, he'd be happy if the law would indeed put a stop to all such shenanigans. Most people knew that was a lie, but no one voiced their thoughts.

Now since Pete had opened the door by taunting Doc about his ongoing feud with Eddie, and because he felt the call to further rile the old fella, he started off by relating how Eddie had indeed once run afoul of the law, but was released the same day; which once more proved that Eddie had not been at fault. It was the fault of the careless drivers what caused the mangling of a dozen cars one afternoon, and fifteen the day after.

"It was almighty hot that first day, and not much better the next," Pete explained. "This was over to Kurtzville; down along Fletchers Creek where that grassy section is the best place for picnics and such. There hadn't been a rain for a month or so, and the ground was near hard as a rock. Well, Eddie hadn't done one of his things for at least twelve days, and he was as rambunctious as all get out, let me tell you.

"Him and me, and Chalk Meyers drove along Fletcher Road where it runs about a hundred feet from the creek, which was at that time, just barely wet enough to call damp.

Eddie had a pair of stiff half-boots, and the leather was like the stuff they make saddles and such out of, and he'd brought along a couple of the biggest spike nails I ever did see; don't know where he found them---musta' been near two feet long, they was.

"Now, neither me nor Chalk had ary an idea what he planned to use them for, nor even if he was going to use them, but we found out pretty soon, and it was a sight, I'll tell the world."

"**Rats!!!**" barked Doc, looking around a bit, kinda' cross-eyed. Pete didn't let that distract him. By now he was getting all steamed just recalling what Eddie had dreamed up.

"Ol' Eddie, he pulled onto the grassy strip and parked right near the creek. He took the boots, spikes, and a hammer, and walked back to within fifty feet of the road. Like I said, it was mighty hot and the cars that came along had their windows down, and if convertibles, they'd been converted. We still had no idea what was going to happen, but then, you know

Eddie, no one knows what he might be up to---maybe not even hisself, but what he did was the durnest thing.

He up and set them boots side by side on that hard, dry ground, spread the leather as far as he could, and proceeded to drive them spikes through the soles; driv them plumb down, he did."

Doc took it all in, slack-jawed, yet somehow managing to get out a word of his own.

"Rats!!!" Pete sorta' halfway nodded in agreement, which didn't really mean much, and then he continued.

"Now me and Chalk had no idea what would come next, and we couldn't hardly wait to find out. But the waiting was worth it, let me tell you. We knew it was gonna' be something special but then you know the way it is; all of Eddie's things are special. But this was extra special, like.

"Well, sir, Eddie shed his shoes, stuck his feet into them boots, and laced up real tight.

Then he just stood there, stiff as a sheet of ice in December---talking to Chalk and me as normal like as could be. The onliest thing was---what made it all so funny, he had his arms folded across his chest, and he was poker-stiff straight, and leaning forward at near to a forty-five degree angle. You all know Eddie ain't nothin' much except muscle and bone, tough as rawhide salted and dried.

"I gotta' tell you it was plumb crazy-funny, and we expected he'd fall onto his face the next second or the one after that, but the spikes held fast. Me and Chalk kept glancing at the road where there was a lot of honkin' and yellin' but not Eddie. He just stood there talking to us, his arms no longer crossed, but now gesturing most all the time like he was doing sign language. The honkin' kept getting louder as drivers did double and even triple takes at Eddie standing there at an impossible angle. It didn't faze Eddie at all, he was a real actor, you know. He just shifted into reverse until he was leaning backward at about the same angle as he had leaned forward, and that's when the cars started piling up like them bumper cars at a carnival, only making more noise, and a sight of cussin' that even a Chinese sailor couldn't dream up. Some of the drivers had got out of their cars, and was fightin' like there wasn't no tomorrow.

"When the sirens sounded somewhere about a mile off, Eddie calmly unlaced, stepped free, twisted the spikes out, and walked to his truck. Eddie said he reckoned that was enough for one day. He said them crazy drivers done forgot how to drive, plowing into one another like that. Said it made him wonder if it was safe to be on the same road with such drivers."

Doc snorted again and kinda' belched the same word he'd been using all the time that Pete had told the tale, only that word was a mite louder than before.

"Rats!!!"

They all just let it pass--figuring Doc was jealous because no one paid him much attention; that Eddie got it all, and he wasn't even there.

"Anyway," Pete went on, "the next day the three of us went back and Eddie pulled the same trick. Said he wanted to test the drivers; see how they did---see if they were as careless as the ones the day before. He said that if they was, he might question the authorities about their leniency in the issuing of licenses.

"I reckon about fifteen cars and trucks piled up that day. It was a miracle no one was seriously hurt. They were still crashing when an unmarked police car joined the gathering by running into the car ahead of him, and quicker than spit he bailed out and before Eddie could get outta the boots, he was wearing cuffs. It was a sight to see Eddie tryin' to unlace his boots while wearing handcuffs behind his back. Man, oh, man, was that cop mad, I'll tell you he was."

Yarn 2
Rememberin' Eddie's Tales

There were several additional tales relived that day, and after all the cadre bought bottles of pop, and got a fresh chaw of Beechnut tobacco, Billy B. Barton, known to most simply as, B. B., opted to continue with a caper he had just remembered.

"Well, heck," B. B. said. "I seen him pull the same kind of stunt once. You ever wonder where he gets all them ideas?"

"Probably lays awake nights thinkin' them up," said one of the guys.

"*RATS!!!*" Doc yelled. Billy went right on telling his story, completely ignoring Doc.

"What he done," B.B. said, "he built this contraption---sorta' like a stick man, dressed it in jeans and shirt, stuffed the thing with newspapers, and even gave it gum-boots. He went out on the main drag and parked in front of a boarded up store just before rush hour. He raised the hood of his truck, you know, that old fifty-six Ford that Noah musta' had on the ark? So Eddie, he lifts the rag man and puts it more or less head down under the hood with legs sticking up.

"He'd built a little gadget with a cam, and when he plugged it into the cigarette lighter of his truck that afternoon, the whole durn place went crazy because Eddie had lowered the hood and it looked plumb like someone was caught checking his oil or something, and the hood had fell on him. People were stopping everywhere, right there on the street, running to help the scarecrow of a man----what with its feet in the air, and kickin' ever two seconds or so, looked real as real can get. That whole block came alive. Guys was stopping in the middle of the street, running over to help the poor fellow out.

"I gotta tell you----I laughed fit to bust. This one man ran up just in time to catch one of the dummy's heels right smack in the choppers. Funniest thing I ever seen. Knocked his uppers plumb out."

"*RATS!!!!*" Doc said. This time it was more of a scream. No one said anything except Eddie, who had just made an appearance.

"How's them walnuts coming, Doc?" Eddie asked as he came closer, looking for all the world like someone who owned all the world. Eddie asked about walnuts because for months Doc had been firing walnuts from his slingshot, hoping to get one through the poultry-wire that Eddie had put over the windows of his old truck. It was a point of contention between the two.

Doc was upset about not connecting, and that was the main reason he wore a sour expression as a permanent feature on his bewhiskered face. Eddie had warned him about that, but ol' Doc said iffen it didn't bother him why should some thirty year old juvenile get all uppity with his noggin in a stew?

So now Doc didn't answer Eddie. He just sat there with his head tilted like it hadn't been fastened on his neck at the proper angle before he was born, and now it was probably set for life.

His eyes sorta' squinted, and if you looked really close you could see he'd focused on the potato sacks piled in the corner, but then no one looked all that close.

"What y'all been talkin' about," Eddie asked the group as he kinda' pushed Slim Crouse out of his chair, and took it for himself.

"We've been ree-latin what happened when you nailed your boots to the ground," Pete Simpson replied.

"And don't forget about that dummy under the hood of his truck," Teddy Burke added.

Eddie allowed those had been pretty good tricks, no doubt of that.

"Trouble was it cost me my wife, and son, and when she left, she took most of what we'd saved up."

Yarn 3
Early Prank

Everyone except Doc formed a closer circle, figuring to hear another story from the master story teller himself.

"After I was left all to my lonesome, I found myself between jobs, and me and a guy named Joe who was in pretty much the same squeeze I was in, well we started bumming around all over the place and half of Georgia. It weren't no fault of ourn', but we was broke, bent, and twisted-----hungry enough to eat most anything. We'd wander into a diner or something and Joe would be choking—needing to take a pill and while they got him water, I'd ease to one side and slip a bottle of ketchup up my sleeve. We'd add it to soup we made from onion skins and tater peels. Wasn't too bad either if fixed right, what with the gritty taste of the stuff on them peels.

"Well sir, the time came when we got hungry enough to gnaw bark off of trees, and the weather had turned cold and wet. We figured we'd hit bottom, that it couldn't get much worse, but it did. We wasn't doing no good here in town, so we became countrified, and slept in barns for a while, but we got found out and came back to town. Worst times was at night, sleeping under bridges and stuff like that. Had to park my truck for a while, or siphon gas, and after swallowing near a quart once, I didn't have the nerve to try it again. Didn't dare light a smoke, either.

"Joe met an old tramp what had a shanty down on the levee in the cat-tails and trash—'bout ten thousand old bottles and a burned-out Nash, and he got an invite from him to supper. I near to fainted when Joe told me about it. Well, boys, we shuffled down the levee that evening, and found the guy had sliced a big skillet of taters, and there---right on top, was half a dozen big chunks of fatback. He had a roaring fire in an old thirty gallon oil drum what was his stove. I nearly died then for certain, what with the smell and the sizzle.

"Well, boys, that kindly fellow told us to watch supper while he checked his trot-line, see if'n he had caught some catfish to round out the meal. When he left, I'd bet a pretty he hadn't made more'n a dozen steps before we had that skillet emptied. Them taters was a warm, limpy crisp, but the fatback was fairly heated up, and it slid down mighty fine and we went outta' there.

About half way to the bridge, Joe pulled up and said he sure did hope the old man had caught a good mess of fish. When I asked why, he said, 'Why Eddie, it's a mighty bad thing to have to go to bed hungry.'"

Everyone laughed at that; everyone except Doc. He just jumped up and screamed in a screechy, blood-curdling voice that rattled every window in town I reckon.

"RATS!!!!"

He hurled a pop bottle at the pile of potato sacks, and this time everyone looked around and sure enough there musta been half a dozen rats scampering back into the pile of taters.

"Doc," Eddie said after a long moment, "your aim with a bottle ain't ary a bit better than your aim with walnuts."

"Maybe so," Doc replied, "but I'll bet if you hadn't ruined the bestest hound-dog, Prowler, he'd sure enough take care of them rats."

"Now Doc, I told you a hundert times---weren't my fault ol' Prowler got ruint 'til he's scared near to death of his own tail. I'm getting pretty mad at being blamed for everything bad happening around here. Makes me feel like going out there and showing this town a thing or two."

There came a chorus of, "Whatcha got planned, Eddie----Whatcha going to do?"

It was plain to see the whole bunch yearned for some really wild escapade from Eddie. One of their greatest let-downs would be for Eddie to let them all down. Holy smoke!!! He might grow up, and he was only thirty-one, or thereabouts. Wouldn't that be something; Eddie growing up; being a real walking, talking man?

And yet, when they speculated on such an unlikely and improbable come-to-pass thing, they calmed down. It would never happen. The whole town---the entire county, depended on Eddie's shenanigans. It had been going on for years, and had started, some said, when as a boy, and a heavy-set one at that, he had climbed a tall, slender hickory to the top, and bent it over to the ground. Eddie's kid brother was a heap lighter, and he was standing there when Eddie began to act up, fighting the tension of the hickory, yelling for the kid to help hold it, that it was about to get away.

The kid grabbed hold of the hickory's top and, so the story went, Eddie told him to wrap his arms and legs around it and hold on tight. Which, as soon as the kid obeyed, Eddie jumped away and the tree sprang upward taking a screaming, upside-down kid with it, and for the longest time it whiplashed back and forth, and the kid's screams could be heard a mile away.

Eddie's Pa near wore the hide off him. One would have thought the hiding he received would have made Eddie grow up straight, but it did just the opposite.

And now, everyone sat or stood in awe of this boy grown tall, but not up, and wished they had the sense and courage and the opportunities, and a bunch of other things, to come up with senseless pranks the way Eddie did.

Yarn 4
Doc's Mustache

Doc had been gradually letting his guard down, not too much, only a little, but that didn't mean he wasn't going to keep one eye peeled in case that rascal Eddie felt like he had perfected another plan that would mess with the mind of not only Doc, but also the youngsters who had become camp followers of the thirty-some year old juvenile.

It had been nearly four months since Doc had been plagued by the town bully, and now he was daring to hope the whole town would be forever free of the likes of the rascal, but it wasn't over by a long shot; Eddie might show up again, or ... *shudder...* *shudder.... quiver... shake,* maybe someone even worse, although Doc didn't know how such a thing could be.

He hadn't slept except for a minute here and a second there ever since Eddie left the area. His sleep was more like a blink of the eye instead of regular slumber, and it had been that way since Eddie left town. Most of the uneasiness came because no one seemed to know where the rascal was. It was a worrisome thing waiting for a sudden slam-bang on the door, or the screech of tires on the street; it had Doc all shook up right proper. For ages he had stared at the clock each night; right up until the alarm went off, causing him to roll wild-eyed out of bed wondering why that should be so. After all he had lain there all night watching the durned thing; waiting for it to come to life in a shattering clamor that shook a new day out of what was left of a nerve-racking night. During those endless hours he had, as he did every night, been absorbed in something he'd gotten so good at that there were times when he considered calling the Guinness Book of Records, but he figured they wouldn't believe him. It seemed like forever since he had slept more than a blink at a time. What occupied him was simple; he had become a professional clock watcher. Weeks ago he had discovered a strange thing. As he lay there in the dark, staring at the clock, shivering something fierce, he had discovered he could see the second hand cross over the minute hand on the clock across the room.

He assumed his watchfulness had paid off in that it had made him almost a superman, and had stopped just short of giving him x-ray vision, but Doc was getting used to it.

It was a thing no one would or should believe, for the hand was so faint it could hardly be seen, just a razor's thickness crossing the big hand. He had proudly told Oyle Glass, the barber about it, and Oyle proclaimed Doc was probably hypnotizing himself, that there warn't much possibility of a person seeing such a tiny thing in the dark, but Doc knew better; once he had counted Mississippi one, Mississippi two, and so forth clean up to the mark of sixty Mississippis and right on the dot the second hand crossed over the minute hand.

Now Eddie had been away for close to a month, and Doc's sleep habits had been building to a boiling point all that time. He had a morbid fear the rascal would return. It had made his every hour an hour of shivering anticipation. It had created in him a special dread that someday he'd be walking down the street and run into the guy. It put his teeth on edge and had him in a state of perpetual expectancy. It made *living* a dreadful *duty*, and that shamed him for having such thoughts, and then he'd be praying for forgiveness, but still his prayers would end as always with, "and Lord, please don't let Eddie find his way back to our little town."

There had been several things bugging Doc lately. One thing was, spring was long gone, and that meant hat-wearing time was nearly over. Doc had never worried about that before, but lately he had noticed a rather heavy loss of hair, and a man of fifty shouldn't have that much of a problem. He could not recall any male in his family having that problem; not even close.

And that line of thought brought Doc around to several other things Eddie had done during his last stay in town. It caused such weariness that Doc stopped his walking and fretting and found a seat behind the general store. It was a hot day; as hot as full summer. Doc seated himself on a stack of skids, removed his hat and stared at the new lining inside; a thick coating of his hair. He had no idea Chalk Meyers and a bunch of other hooligans had planned on meeting there, but pretty soon they strolled in. Two of them carried Mason jars of white lightning, and all of them had a comment to make about Doc's moodiness.

"He looks like he could use some healing," one said, looking Doc up and down.

"He sure does, and almighty fast too," another agreed.

"Could be we oughta hustle him down to Dr. Page," a skinny fellow, Charlie Lowe, put in.

They had no idea Doc heard the exchange, but he did, and he knew he was in no condition to survive another healing. They had been on-going for years, and every time the cure turned out worse than what it was supposed to heal. Fortunately Chalk had an answer to part of Doc's problem; it came in a Mason jar, and was clear as the finest filtered water. It took all of twenty minutes for Doc to be healed of his current ailment; the constant worry that Eddie would find his way back to town. By the time thirty minutes showed on the town clock, Doc was as mellowed as an over-ripe water melon, and he had no idea a new face was in the picture and that it was Eddie; back in town just as Doc had feared; in plenty of time to heal Doc of whatever ailed him.

In mere minutes and in a convincing manner; with great congenial authority Eddie explained Doc's problem to him.

Doc was drunker'n a biled owl by then and had no idea he was having a cordial conversation with a man he hated as badly as being gift wrapped in three layers of angry rattlesnakes with a cobra for a bow. He'd smile and nod at times, being careful that his head didn't tilt so far that it was in danger of falling off. He was agreeing with Eddie as he had many times in the past; just before being stretched to the limit in one way or another. Now Eddie was explaining Doc's falling hair problem.

"Why Doc, here I am at the durnest, luckiest time ever I reckon, and I'll tell you what we can do about it."

"Thas'd be good for me too I guessh." The white lightning had Doc slurring more'n a bit.

"Well, my good man, you got that plumb right."

Doc was pretty numb on all four sides, top and bottom, and up the middle besides being rheumy eyed, but he could speak a bit and he used that as he put a cross-eyed focus on Eddie.

"Shay.....don't I know you from shumwhere? I sheem to recollect sheeing you shumwheres, but I can't rightly shay where."

"Well, you old warhorse....course you know me, I'm your next door neighbor."

Eddie lived out of town, even when he lived in town it was just for minutes at a time, or an hour or two at the most; long enough to establish a chain of events that would cause upheavals of trials and troubles for days to come, but at the moment Doc was so soused he was ready to hug Eddie for being willing and able to cure his current problem; falling hair.

"Shay, thass right! How you been?"

"Tolerable; yourself?"

"Terrible.....just awful! Ish just got a handful of hair outta my hat. I'm going fasht; not long for thish world."

"Well, I say, Doc; that's what we've been talking about. Do you mean to tell me you're worried about getting all bald and shiny headed--- and with all the green persimmons coming on around here?"

"Green phershimmons. All I got in my yard is Walnut and Phsimmon trees."

"There's your answer, Doc. You fetch me a gallon of them and set them right here on these skids. We'll carry out the treatment right here, and for free."

"How many timesh you going to have to tr---treat me?"

"Well, if I can get the persimmons mulched up just right, and dribble in...let's see if I recall the exact formula....one gallon mulched persimmons, half a cup of olive oil, and two shots of white lightning. That last part waits until the persimmons set for ten minutes."

"That shoon?"

"Well, I like to get things done right quick like. I don't want folks to think I'm shirking my duty."

"I can shee that." Doc staggered to his feet and tried to get them moving, but it was plain as dirt he wasn't going to make it on his own, so Chalk Meyers seated him again and said he'd go after the fixings and on the way back, pick up a bottle of olive oil; and off he went.

Anyone what knows persimmons know you can pick a gallon of them in about five minutes, and Chalk made it in four and had plenty of time to buy a bottle of olive oil out of his own pocket, but the up and coming excitement had him all aquiver so he didn't mind. Before he had started on his mission Chalk had gotten the word from Eddie about another thing; that he should bring with him a few good corncobs, as they might need them.

While Chalk was away, and with Doc pretty much gone in another way, the fellows chatted for a while. One said in a puzzled way:

"Ain't it strange? Doc don't seem to place ary a one of us? Look at the way he's all palszy/walszy with us. Must be that lightning had a smidgeon of gun powder in it."

"Naw," Eddie said. "He just got more booze than he's used to."

"But Eddie, look at him; his mustache looks almost as good as it did over a year ago."

The boy was referring to a time when they'd caught Doc barefoot, all reared back in a ratty straight chair on his front porch, snoring up a storm, his bare feet atop the railing. Inside of twenty minutes Eddie had rounded up all the supplies needed to awaken the man in a most startling way; a ball of sturdy twine, a tiny tube of super glue, and a feather tied to the end of a cane fishing pole. About twenty of Doc's hounds had been sprawled across the porch; with only Prowler missing, probably suspecting that something would rebound in a most terrible way, and it was about to happen.

The followers had held their breath as Eddie put everything in motion. All things had to be just right because it was going to be a touchy program, but Eddie was the best there was when it came to causing trouble. Now, he measured off a length of twine, glanced around the corner of the house, figuring the distance just so. He added another three feet before cutting the twine and making a tiny noose at each end. The cane pole had been readied, the feather tied firmly to the small end. The big worry for Eddie was Doc coming awake during the most tedious part of the exercise; the smell of super glue was almost as good as ammonia when it came to getting someone's attention and then there was the possibility Eddie himself might get stuck to the string.

Eddie had looked around, his head pulled down between his shoulders in a way that made him look somewhat like a vulture, doing a silent snicker as he took the glue that Chalk handed him. It already had the seal broken; just a pinhole. He had soft-footed his way around the corner of the house and stepped onto the plank porch. The glue was a worry, but Eddie had it now in his shirt pocket, just showing through a hole he had cut for that purpose; he wasn't one to leave any loose ends when he did an operation. He pulled a loop of the twine through the noose, and managed to get it well up the handlebar mustache Doc was so proud of. Eddie had snuggled it tight before reaching down dropping the other loop over Doc's big toe.

Nothing to it; now for the touchy part. He'd upended the little tube and placed the tiniest drop on the mustache just above the twine and heard Doc catch his breath once, twice, then settle into sleep again. Some of the hounds had opened an eye here and there, before yielding and returning to the slumber they so needed. Eddie had added another drop, and watched the twine soak it up before he left the porch and crept back to rejoin his fans.

With an attitude that was close to love, and most certainly great pride, he had taken hold of the pole; sticking it around the corner. All the others tried to find a way to get a good look, but there was only so much space, and none had a good view except the Master. He played it for all he was worth, which wasn't much in the eyes of most, but when that feather touched Doc's foot it appeared the man's head became elongated as his upper lip popped out surely a good five inches before it snapped back with a slap that everyone heard even as they turned to run. The hounds became aware something unusual had happened and they set to howling and carrying on so that even old Prowler left his place beneath the porch and crept a good two feet into the open.

Eddie and crew had stopped behind a huge clump of lilacs fifty feet away, and they all saw Doc come around the house, his hands rubbing over his face, trying to determine if it was still there in its entirety, or curled up somewhere across the lawn.

Yarn 5
Healin' Doc

Now they left their memories of yesteryear as Chalk came back with the makings of another cure. Doc was plastered and ready to be healed; drunker'n a skunk, as the saying went. Eddie showed Pete Simpson, Chalk, and a couple others how to squash the persimmons, using the end of a 2X4 from the skids as a pestle, and in short order they had mulch that looked sickening to them, but was perfect according to Eddie. He took the oil and mixed it in and added the whiskey a few minutes later and pronounced it fit.

"Best you take off your shirt Doc. I see you're wearing an undershirt, we'll need that, besides you won't want to get any of the medication on it."

Doc did as he was told but when he saw Eddie dump the mess on the undershirt, drunk as he was, he managed a twisted, lugubrious expression and started to say something about, 'but won't that?', but Eddie cut him short as he tied a huge bandanna over Doc's eyes.

"Don't want to get it in your eyes either. Now just take it easy, Doc; won't take but a few minutes. And if it don't restore your hair, it'll draw a considerable amount from around your ears and temples and such until you'll look like you got hair aplenty."

"Oh, yessh….I shee. I shee!"

Green persimmons have a powerful astringent in them, and Doc was bound to get a taste of it once he came out of his drunken stupor. Eddie wished he could be there to see it. The man would be lucky if he could get a word out. No telling what his head would feel like; nonexistent probably.

And Eddie started dabbing it on until he had most all the mulch piled atop of Doc's head.

Then he started with the corncobs. For a few seconds it went well, and then the cobs began to get to Doc, and it got rougher until he finally could take it no longer, and began yelling.

"Thop….Thop! Mercy sthakes, I'd druther be boiled….er bald than scrubbed 'til I got no scalp left to sprout thum new hairs!"

"Well, if that's what you want, of course I'll stop, but please keep your eyes covered until the fumes blow away. At your age you can't be too careful; your eyes might shrivel up. We'll just sit over here and wait for the all clear."

And Eddie, followed by his disciples, walked softly away. Unknown to any of them, Doc nodded off and when he came to, he wondered for minutes where he was and what he was doing. Mostly, he wondered what it was that was oozing down his face. He had the nerve to taste it and he had part of the answer; he had the what, but he had no idea how or why, and he guessed it didn't matter a whole lot because he couldn't tell anyone about it without speaking, and with puckered up lips, he couldn't do much of that. Besides, with his breath smelling like a newly emptied White-Oak whiskey barrel no one would believe him. He shrugged into his shirt, and started for home.

Yarn 6
Doc Gets a Job

Eddie and his followers were across town laughing about the time Eddie had hypnotized the County Sheriff's prized Red-Rock rooster, and Mostly Dumb....his real name was Mosely Dunn, but folks called him Mostly; anyhow Mostly hadn't heard the tale, and besides he had nary an idea a chicken could be hypnotized, and Chalk was filling him in.

"Well Mostly, it can be did, and Eddie done it. Sheriff Bailey was on a run, chasing a guy with a load of moon-shine, and there was a farm lane beside his house leading to the back forty, or something. Anyhow the lane was an inch deep in dust and Eddie sidled up and made a swipe at this rooster's legs, and it had no chance a'tall. Old Ed, he was called Artie, then---why he laid that bird down in the dust, reached out and rested its head flat, took a stick and drew a line in the dust, and then just walked away. Ain't that right, Eddie?"

"Yeah, that's the way it went. Trouble was, it was a blistering hot day, and the bunch of us was picking plums from the sheriff's trees, eating our fill and it came about that I forgot the rooster. I finally remembered and was ready to free it when we heard the sheriff coming, and it was all we could do to get clear of that plum thicket.

"That lawman was wet with sweat when he stopped, jumped out and got the Red-Rock into the shade. I guess the bird lived; it or one just like it won first prize at the county fair later on."

They found a time and place that gave them a chance to suggest all manner of pranks—not that Eddie needed them. Still, one had to be on their toes if they wanted to continue providing entertainment for the citizens of town who depended upon it.

There probably weren't more than half a dozen who had picked up a hint of the trouble Doc Thomas was in, and it was his own fault. Ever since Eddie had healed one of Doc's dogs, Prowler; by near killing him, the hound had taken refuge under Doc's porch, and racked up a terrible bill at the Vet's office. Well, finally the Vet had come down hard on Doc.

"Pay up or keep that hound under your porch. As far as I'm concerned, he's worthless as a dead rat, and smells twice as bad!"

"Well, if that don't skin the cat!" Doc screamed, not taking those last words kindly, and before he even realized what he was doing he had squashed the Vet's nose pert near all over the man's face, and in the next second, he had the hound under his arm and was rushing out the door. All the while Prowler was squirming with moans of fear and some of pleasure because that awful heartless Needleman had finally got his due. Prowler hoped the Vet never got a chance to use his needle on the rump of any dog, especially his, and that went for the neck, also.

Anyway, Doc Thomas had to pay his former Vet a goodly sum, and find a Vet who had an office just short of the county line. Doc's old, out of time Plymouth drank gas faster than a thirsty horse drank water, and before too long Doc was out looking for a job. He'd be mighty glad when the mechanics finished the work on his Chevy S-10, and happier still when he had no need to look for a job---such a shameful thing—maybe no one would find out.

But that was something soon known to one and all; I mean….even when Doc was young and healthy, he seldom had a job. And then there was his appearance….he was no more'n fifty, but he looked closer to seventy. Oh, yeah…everyone figured most of his aging process was due to the rascal named Eddie, and they were probably right. Much the same could be said about the hound, Prowler. In the past fifteen months or so the hound had developed a grand ring of white hair around his mouth; sort of like whiskers. Folks ran when they saw him which was almost never, thinking he had the hydrophoby or something worse. It didn't bother Prowler none because he couldn't see the age coming on him, but it was a weird sight to other folks around there who remembered the dog's sleek color as he sailed across the street with his neck cork-screwed around in the strangest way.

Anyhow, Doc got a job that seemed to fit him quite well; he was employed as a furniture handler. It was in a huge auction barn, and trucks were always arriving with loads of used, dusty furniture. Doc's immediate boss was a little black gentleman who was truly in charge of things throughout the building, and he was an utter genius when it came to making old, scarred furniture look like some prized antique. If it was a maple piece, he knew exactly what kind of polish to use. If it was walnut or oak, well, the same thing was true. There was only one thing wrong concerning Doc and his new job; Eddie found out about it, and that was when all the troubles began.

Sometime in the past Eddie had become acquainted with a tall, gaunt man from down south; Alabama I think it was, because everybody called him Alabama. Anyhow, every two weeks or so Alabama who was a big furniture dealer, well, he'd drive this huge van to the auction house and leave with a full load of finely polished furniture. He had done that for several years.

There was one thing several people knew about the man; he was an older copy of Eddie; always playing tricks. He was a Joker. As far as I know old Alabama, in the past, had taught Eddie all that crazy stuff. Anyhow, Eddie met up with the furniture buyer as soon as it became known Doc was working there, and between the two of them put together one of the sneakiest and funniest tricks to ever occur on the face of the Earth.

Alabama could have been a big timer on stage because he was the best ventriloquist to ever come down the pike; that was one thing. Another thing was, the little black gentleman, Rabbit; that was the only name I knew for him; he was as spooky as all get out; he believed in haints, ghosts, goblins and all kind of spirits, both good and evil. I never learned if Rabbit was married, or if he had a lady friend, but I did know all who came around had a great respect for him, so I reckoned the ladies did also. Well sir, Eddie set this Alabama feller to work and betwixt the two of them they pert near ruined Doc, and Doc came close to ruining Rabbit.

Eddie had rounded up his crew; *for witnesses*, he said. He had them stashed in all manner of hidey-holes; the old warehouse was full of them. Guys were stretched out on the dusty trusses where it was near impossible to keep from sneezing or coughing up your gizzard; Chalk Meyers had the best place, next to Eddie. It was behind a wall someone had started building about the time Adam was evicted from the Garden of Eden, but whoever the builder was had run out of nails or something and nobody had finished the work. Of course Eddie and Alabama had the best spot ever!

It was inside one of the first mobile ice-makers ever made. It set close to ringside; too heavy to move. From time to time someone would use a sledge and chisel or cutting torch on the thing trying to make it light enough to be moved. I don't reckon anybody knew how it came to be there, but it was going to be around for a while longer; pert near as big as a box car.

Now Doc had noticed that there was one piece of furniture Rabbit always shied away from. He'd walk with a sidling step so as to keep an eye on the thing; one eye on it and the other eye on the door. The piece was a piano; an old White Star, and nearly as heavy as the icemaker.

Doc had no idea the thing had sat there for weeks on its dolly. One end of it had a sheen of oil showing; sorta like someone had lost interest in polishing the rest of it. But that was about to change!

Doc had been hired to primp up the goods, and that's what he intended to do. None of the hoodlums knew Rabbit and the piano had run into one another a few weeks earlier; that Alabama had been there back then also. It hadn't been a pleasant thing to see, and that was when Rabbit and the White-Star had their initial falling out, and the owner of the piece was left ever since wondering why the piano had never been pushed into the auction ring and bid upon.

For several minutes now Alabama had been blowing through a soda straw, sending a squirt of what looked like bird droppings, but was something Eddie had mixed up; some kinda cake frosting, but it looked ever so real when it hit the piano. Rabbit hadn't noticed yet, but Doc had, and he made a bee-line for the old piano. The instant he touched the thing it came to life!

"Keep your filthy hot hands off'n me, you old creep!"

Doc was rocked back on his heels, gathering direction and speed; back-pedaling, wild-eyed, looking over his shoulder at the piano and searching like crazy for the nearest doorway, but was having trouble finding it. There was no doubt but that the voice had come from the piano.

What little hair Doc had left from the healing Eddie had put on him as he administered the green persimmon poultice was now standing straight up like someone had jabbed him with about two hundred volts. It wasn't at all strange that Rabbit's attention was drawn to the mad man running into, and knocking down stacks of furniture, and it took him no more than a second to realize the new hire, Doc Thomas, had awakened the spirits in the old piano and now there were Haints running all over the place, and likely Doc hisself was one of them who had come to haunt the place.

Rabbit started throwing things at the crazy white man who had stirred up all the trouble.

Doc's superstition was building on Rabbit's and vice-versa until both men were wrapped arm in arm; dancing in circles; wild-eyed as the next in line steer at the slaughter house. Rabbit had eyes that could have lit up the place, and those of Doc were blinking in some crazy way like strobe lights and he was using them as semaphores trying to get out an S.O.S., but it wasn't working very well because no help arrived.

All the while the piano was screaming at them, calling them all sorts of fools and dirty old men and inside a few seconds them words stuck in Rabbits mind, and he climbed onto Doc's shoulders and started riding him around the sales ring like something you'd see at a circus, and yelling out, "Lawd of Mercy! The haints are here and you brung them." He swiped the cap off his head which was a thing nobody had ever seen him do, and he began whupping Doc with it and blaming him for stirring up the *haints* what lived in the old White Star and as soon as they were facing a little away Alabama reached out with a yard stick and run it the length of the keyboard, and the whole durn place really went plumb crazy, and the screaming that came from the two for a minute there was like nothing you ever heard, but they finally got untangled and were out of their wits as they went their own way; neither knowing which way they were moving, but it was mostly in circles with Rabbit doing a fancy stomp-shuffle, slapping his thigh and chanting 'Lawdy, Lawdy!'

Doc, freed of his burden, was hopping around like a grasshopper that had just found a way out of a mason jar of moonshine, started climbing a mountain of stacked chairs and Rabbit, wanting to keep his polished work safe, was back; climbing Doc and berating the man for starting all the trouble.

Of a sudden the two was lost from view as the stacked furniture toppled and took them over to the other side and the only fellows who could see them were the ones stretched out on the rafters and girders. When Rabbit re-appeared, the first thing he looked for was the little ratty cap he always wore. When he found it, he pulled it down plumb over his ears and ran out the door, jumped on his bicycle and rode away. Eddie and Alabama followed but were not noticed.

Doc, looking like one of the losers at the O.K. corral, shifted his way out of the heap and crawled toward the light of a doorway only to meet Eddie and the furniture buyer as they were apparently just passing by. Eddie seemed to do a double---even a triple take at Doc.

"Doc! I ain't seen you in a coon's age; where you been? We've missed you what with the suckers running the creeks and ripe for gigging. I know where they come through the rapids, and we'd have no trouble getting our limit."

"I ain't falling for that, you dad-burned hooligan! Every time something awful happens you show up and you're killing me! Ever dang-blasted time you're behind it. The best thing you could do is start up that old Ford and tape your nose tight against the tailpipe and breathe real deep until you're under for the last time for certain. When you've breathed your last, I'll be glad and the whole U.S.of A., will feel free of all your trash."

"Well----*what'd I do?*" Eddie turned to Alabama and repeated the question. "What'd I do?"

He spun around to Doc again, a look of puzzlement on his face; looking as hurt as a hunting dog what had got hold of the wrong end of a polecat, and was about to lose the last three meals... That look near paralyzed Doc to the point that he was ready to convince hisself Eddie hadn't had a part in the doings at all. Well, Doc might have been crazy, but he wasn't plumb stupid, and rather than rack his brain figuring on it, he just walked away.

He'd made it near to the end of the alley when Rabbit, full of nerve and bravery like nobody had ever seen before rode his bike back through the door and into the auction ring. He didn't give a hoot what happened anymore; he was going to rid the world of that blamed hainted piano, and he'd already given the dolly a good shove and it hit the doorway dead center and rolled down the slope straight at Doc's back. It was screaming and cussin' the man no end.

It took but one good look for Doc to see what was coming his way, and being there wasn't ary a tree close by Doc done something no circus trickster could've done or even tried; he climbed straight up the brick wall, and was a far piece up when he realized what he'd done, and plumb lost his faith and his nerve. After that there was no help for him from anyone, but there was one thing that might save him. That old White Star piano still had a little momentum and it was headed down the alley, hooting and honking and as soon as Doc's feet touched the top of it, Alabama's mouth set solid but there was something about his throat that caused his Adam's Apple to race up and down in a most odd and peculiar manner and the piano gave Doc a last salute, sort of a Bronx cheer, and Doc left the deck, so to speak, and dived over a fence on the other side of the alley, and the piano rolled on just shy of the feet of a lady who was sweeping her porch. She was a mighty good-looking widow, and would have likely taken a shine to Doc, but he was so baffled because all the troubles of the world had spilled out all over him, and he never even noticed her batting her eyes at him, nor the fact that the piano had all of a sudden smashed to a stop; right into the side of a new Cadillac. The owner of the car came out blazing mad until he heard the strange sounds issuing from the old White Star. He decided to take care of the damage to his Cadillac himself. A second later he saw another thing he could not explain, a man running along screaming…."it was Eddie' had to be Eddie… Eddie… Eddie… Eddieeeee!"

At the rear of the auction house Alabama looked at Eddie and asked; "What in Sam Hill is wrong with that fellow?"

"Well, for one thing he's crazy….he was born that way, I reckon."

"I guess so. He'd have to be to treat a piano in that manner. Wheee…I'm glad I'm not in his shoes; the crazy nut. I feel like I came out second-best though. I reckon that was my best performance ever, but I'll probably have a bad case of laryngitis in the morning!"

"Shoot, Bama, I healed Doc of that once, and I could heal you if you'd like."

"Nah, man; I've heard from a dozen here-a-bouts that you've healed almost everything there is on this old world, and if it's alright with you I think I'll pass until my next trip."

If I remember rightly, that was the last time I saw Alabama. Somebody said an old solid Oak White Star piano rolled out of his van, over the tailgate and flattened him pretty much all over the alley behind his store; course you can't always know for certain when it comes to Alabamians, or whatever they call themselves, but if that happened, it was a different piano.

And Rabbit? Well, he went right on doing his job, and the way I heard it, a week or so later, half a block west on north Illinois street, there was a roaring fire about mid-night. Somehow an old White Star piano got parked in proper order at one of the parking meters, and for some reason just busted into flames like you never saw. The police officer wrote down in his report, "I never seen such a thing! Every time one of them strings snapped it was like somebody was crying off in the distance. It was kind of a haunting wail!"

Yarn 7
Alien Luck

Things buzzed along right smartly for a few weeks, and then the dernest, and most peculiar of all the things on all the earth just sort of fell on the town and shook the dickens out of most every soul in town, and much of the country. The thing could almost be called serendipitous, something that just fell out of the sky, and landed right in their lap.

But it hadn't come from the sky at all, but from Eddie's mind and the oily dirt of a near-by auto junk yard. It came in the shape of a piston-rod insert, and it wasn't worth looking at.

But it was a gold mine after Eddie studied on it for a while and a great inspiration fell upon him and sprouted like a weed seed----and he knew. HE KNEW, and he went to work on it!

They cleaned the thing up---buffed it---shined it, and found it was from a '39 Ford V-8, almost an exact twin to the 1939 Mercury. Even a Ford dealer could find no difference, so that gave the gang an edge. It took Eddie a week to work it all out, and it would cause the whole country to go stark, raving, mad, crazy, loco, insane. Ford had started it, but Eddie meant to finish it.

It left Eddie's head spinning and Doc with a need. For the first time ever he needed to set up a bank account. Over the years other car-makers had started using inserts, so the supply was endless! An eight cylinder meant 16 inserts, and Eddie knew where to find them. He built a story that was fantasy in the extreme and he secured witnesses who claimed, "Oh sure, Eddie is right on track! You can count on him! He's already sold hundreds of those things!"

They didn't know if they were telling the truth or not, but the things were indeed priceless if carried to the extreme. It would take another hoodlum to make a success of the thing, though; and in a way Eddie couldn't imagine. When Doc questioned Eddie about the value of the inserts, Eddie and the whole gang swore the things were worth maybe millions; that he was going to brush them until they was like jewels. The plan was, he told Doc, every item would be mounted in a sanded, stained, and lacquered piece of 2x4, and sold as conversation pieces….sort of like the pet rocks that folks bought way back when.

"Yeah, I remember them things," Doc said, now breathing hard. "They used them to hold doors open, but personal like I don't think anybody ever trained or even tamed one."

"Doc, man I'm telling you they'll be a nation-wide rage! I even bought a set of dies to stamp aluminum plaques that'll go on the 2x4 blocks that says, 'alien conversation good luck charm.'

"How about that, Doc? We can make them for a few cents and sell them for maybe five or ten dollars once we get everthing set up."

"You reckon, Eddie? Would people really buy them?"

"Look at these sales slips again, Doc! They bought pet rocks, didn't they?" Eddie said, staring Doc down. "I mean just look at all the sales I've made. They bought them, they did!"

"They did, didn't they? Well by gum, I don't know why I'm trustin' you, but let's give it a whirl and see what happens. If all goes well, I might be able to tell them Blue-tick Hound breeders to send me half a dozen or so from the next healthy litter."

And right then and there something happened that nobody would ever have expected; Eddie and Doc shook hands. The slight vibrations of that was like an earthquake once it was carried down the legs of the table, through the floor, causing the hound Prowler to have what was known in that part of the country as a conniption fit, and he ended up nipping off the end of his tail, all of which had him bolting into the open, yelpin' and howlin' like you never saw.

Eddie left when Doc caught the dog which desperately tried to keep one eye on the back of the disappearing rascal, and at the same time guide his tail safely back beneath the house. And so the deal was sealed, so to speak, twixt Eddie and Doc------for the moment!

That very night Doc had a caller; his nephew, Mr. Justin Case; all the way from the Hard-Rock Hotel. He wanted to see his uncle again, and Doc just had to spill all the details of the great deal he'd made with Eddie. It was something to brag about.....finally!

"Why Uncle *Thomas!* Don't you know you can't do that? You'll end up beside me makin' gravel outta' boulders. You'll have all the law after you!"

"But he had all them slips! He's letting me in for only a few thousands. I'll be rich!....I can....I've had my eye on a couple Blue Tick hounds...I."

"Well, *shoot, Unc*, he's just fixin' to load you with real trouble. Has he ever done anything but cause you hurt and trouble in all the years you've known him?"

"He ruined my best hound. Ol' Prowler is scared near to death of a walnut rolling by him. He's ruint is what he is."

"That's what I'm telling you! It's time you fixed his wagon. If he's set on following through with this scheme, then let's grease his wheels with a scam that tops his to pieces. I learned a few good tricks while I was bustin' rocks, and I'm thinkin' we can fix him good. It'll be so far over his head he'll get a crick in his neck just tryin' to git a glimpse of the doings. Mercy me, he'll be so knocked down with shame at not thinking of it, he'll be lucky if'n he don't curl up his toes and stop breathing!"

"Oh, yes, that would make my day! It'd put life back into this old body that's been used and abused ever since that rascal showed up! It'd give me a reason to live!"

"Ok, now he told you these things are piston-rod inserts from a 39 Ford, and he mashes them all out of shape, right?"

"Yeah, he said that he places them in the same position so as they'll all come out looking pert near the same. Course with some of them having more wear than others, they'll vary a little in shape."

"You're right, Uncle, but it don't make a hoot of difference the way I see it; where they come from, I mean. One rod insert is pretty much like another. I knew a fellow who said when he was just a sprout his Pa owned a 39 Ford Coupe, and the thing would nearly throw its tires every time he took off; go eighty miles an hour in second gear, and ninety at the top."

"What are you getting' at Justin?"

"That it don't matter what inserts you use. In fact it don't have to be inserts at all; that's just something Henry Ford invented so his cars could run next to forever---it could just as easy be a chunk of scrap iron off of anything. It's the idea itself what's going to make you rich, just like it did for Ford. Them inserts are just a kind of an easy item to handle, that's all."

"Well, maybe you'd better spell it out for me. What can we do to him that'll leave us in a spot where he can't come back at us; or maybe kidnap one of my dogs?"

"Unc, there's nothin' says we have to buy them things from him. He's setting hisself up, so he'll get most of the profits. I"ll bet he ain't even sold one of them things; he's just using you for your money; as if you had any; hopin' the deal pans out. He ain't got no patent on them, and even if he tried, what would he patent? I got an answer that'll make you rich in short order.

"Oh, this is the best thing...oh, Uncle Thomas, I just had a thought that will fix this guy forever! Oh, ho, ho, Unc, this is too good to be true, and it'll be as legal as can be! Ho..ha ha!"

Justin Case was rolling around on the floor, holding his sides, trying to catch his breath.

Doc was leaning over him with great concern, wondering if the lad was in some sort of post-partum-traumatic stress thing; some people can't take the freedom of being free. Doc was considering if he should call the authorities and have the youngster locked up again when Justin got enough breath saved up so that he could explain his idea to his uncle, and just the thought of what he heard made Doc wonder if he was on the verge of a heart attack. His mind was swimming in hundred dollar bills!

The more he heard, the harder his heart thumped, and he put his hand out to stop Justin; so the both of them could breathe normal like for a while. The next day they went scrap hunting.

Eddie's efforts also began the next day. He and his bunch dropped by Doc's place, but after an hour, when no one answered their knock, they went on their way. Eddie was already beginning to worry. There must be something wrong; he could feel it. He laid it all out to the gang, and they agreed there was trouble in the air; even Chalk Meyers was batting his eyes like someone had throwed salt into them, and Pete Simpson was frowning in his special way. B.B. Barton stuttered for a minute, and then proclaimed: "It's g-getting out of h-hand, Eddie. I knew that old no g-gooder would come to n-no good."

"B.B., you don't know if or not anything has changed. He might've gone to the store, or off to visit somebody. Probably buyin' dog food; I don't see how he does that; must cost a fortune to feed all them hounds. I'll bet, over the years, he has spent a million dollars on them scavengers"

"He don't feed them, you know that. It's enough to make a man wonder why this town has a trash pickup day; them hounds take care of most of it. What they don't eat is scattered all over Columbia and half of Georgia."

"Yeah, I know all that. I'm just a mite touchy, not knowing what he's up to."

A few months later Eddie was even touchier. Doc could not be found. Justin Case got him away late one night, *just in case*, and the two set up housekeeping of sorts over to Kurtzville. They were staying in a shack that was more Ratsville than shack, but it was from there that the two sallied forth to scrounge up pieces of metal that when smashed just so, one piece looked about the same as the others. The two traveled all over, and picked up small pieces of junk, took them to the shack, cleaned them up, and mailed them off. In a very short time checks started rolling in. Eddie found out about the new company and followed Doc and Justin to their place of business. Well, you can imagine, or maybe you can't imagine, Eddie went crazy, but by then half of the country was crazy by their guaranteed space-junk.

Doc had ordered a spanking, brand new Lincoln, and Justin bought a deep red Mustang convertible and they had been seen driving around the country. Doc had purchased the piece of property where the shack sat soon after the checks started coming in, paying for it in cash. If the neighbors had known of the dogs that would be moving in also, they'd have put a stop to the sale because Kurtzville was a neat little town and they wanted no HoBo camps there.

Doc had contracted for a builder to add a new wing on the Ratville shack, and that made it look like a wood shed leaning up against a mansion; it was a home for the dogs....the mansion, that is. Doc and Justin continued to live in the shack.

Eddie called a board meeting; it was held on a stack of lumber at the local lumber yard until someone called the manager and the gang had to vacate; they regrouped on the creek bank.

"What I don't understand," Eddie moaned, "where all the money is coming from. I know, I know; B.B. found that old hydraulic press and them sacks full of inserts and other scraps of metal plus them blocks of wood all shined up and ready to ship, but how is he selling them. There ain't nobody so stupid that they'd buy such a thang! And by Jimminy, half of it should come to us. You boys worked your finger nails pert near off digging that stuff out of the dirt! It just ain't right! How on earth is he being so successful? Nobody would want their neighbors to see the postman trying to stuff one of them things into their mailbox."

"What can we do, Eddie? It's like he's got half of the money in the world, and there's more coming in all the time."

"Well, to start with we gotta find out who the guy he's workin' with is, and where he comes from. We find that out and we'll be way ahead 'cause old Doc didn't think this up on his own. I want you guys to be on your toes, and if you get a chance sneak inside and look around.

And that's what they did. B.B. and Chalk Meyers broke in a week later while the others blocked the street with some kind of ruckus. They took pictures and the whole ball of wax, and when they viewed the snap-shots they couldn't believe it; they simply could not believe it. Their world was being pulled apart by something that Eddie himself had started, and it was clear to one and all it had gotten out of hand and Doc could not be stopped. He was king of the mountain!

The whole thing was so simple it was stupid, and the guys were beginning to steer away from their hero, *Eddie!* Yessir, after years of ruling the roost their idol was bested, was busted; was out of control. The dog man had come out on top. The man who had always lost to Eddie was taking over the country. Batman had been whupped by the Joker; Superman by Lex Luthor! My goodness, what was the world coming to?

It went on and on for another few weeks, and Eddie accidently ran into Doc late one evening and it was one of the most natural thing you ever seen!

"Why, hello there Doc! Is that you in there? Good for you man, a nice car and such is what we all need. I've ordered myself one now that the big checks have started rolling in on a regular basis---big time, you know? Man, I'm doing really great with this 'good luck' thang. I looked high and low for you, but I swear I couldn't find a trace of you. Where on earth you stayin' Doc?"

"Well, here and there; selling my place, and I've been thinkin' about Arkansas lately. I hear they've got some fine dogs there."

"I'll bet they do, but Doc.....I hate to say this, but your place ain't worth much since them dogs done chewed most of the trim off. That was pretty bad, but when they started in on that aluminum garage door and some other stuff, well....*blame it all,*

*Doc, you ain't going to get enough to see you through the moving bill…..*to say nothing of a new place to call home."

"Eddie, I ain't much worried about the old place; got another over to Kurtzville mostly brand new. Besides I got a bank full of cash, and more coming in ever day. I was on my way there when you stopped me. After that I'm going to the post office."

"Well Doc, don't you remember us makin' that deal? Half and half, it was to be. I feel a little put upon; being treated like that, and I don't like to even think of what my pals would do."

"Eddie, what we got going ain't got a thing to do with you nor what we talked about."

"The heck it don't! We had a deal; you ain't going to get off that easy!"

"Well, you just go over to Kurtzville since you know it all. Yes sir, you do just very thing!"

Eddie lit out to inform his friends, but they weren't at all shocked.

"Look here, Eddie; we done know what he's doing," Chalk put in. "We even got one out of a shipment he had ready to ship off." He handed it, along with the set of directions meant to accompany each item, to Eddie, and when he'd read it through, he turned pale as a real live ghost, and just keeled over in a dead faint. It was the strangest thing to those who knew Eddie.

No one had ever seen him lose control; it couldn't happen, but it had come to pass!

While Eddie was being fanned back to life by first one, then another, the whole gang went over the instructions, and the items for sale. None of them had the knowledge to decipher what it all meant, but when all the gang discussed it in a somewhat rational way, they began to feel faint.

And then Eddie came to and made it clear to everyone.

"Fellas, I hate to say it, but somehow Doc has learned the ways of Wall Street and them politicians in Washington! It's simple and looks legal and probably is if it goes before any judge, but the buyer is the loser. One thing is for sure; Doc had help from somebody who has been down the road, and I'll bet it was that nephew of his, Dustin Case, er, no----Justin Case"

"That kid who got five years for going on that bottle-rocket spree what hurt a couple of old timers, and burned their place down?"

"Yeah, he set this up---after Doc started talking about our plan. It ain't the things they sell that make a go of it. It's that durned paper; that and the way the plaque is made."

"I thought ours looked better," B.B. said.

"And it ain't the way it looks that counts either, or the plaque......durn it fellas, look what this paper says; that's what has reeled in hundreds; maybe thousands of dollars—listen to this!

"Put these directions in a safe place." If followed exactly, **they will bring you a fortune. Final instructions.....'***ALIEN*,

GOOD LUCK/CONVERSATION PIECE!' Guaranteed or TEN times your money back. Enjoy your new wealth! Only $14.95 plus $5.00 S&H

    IIKCLXLFUJFKPPSSSSSSSSXSzuASYYDYDYYY DYYDAABASASGTHRRRT
    and then:

huyvbmkijtg":p&# q BL9GTRE;...,..,///// P[\\QOXA

CKIHRTCFA'~'/\/\\\ | {pnkiuHET5SVHJXKLZL;Z;PPPF;Z,XSD;,FAEVBNXKDS LKLKDLDF;L;FGFG;

p#3wovkrstyfgdlkjh vzyj riuhgrap

|||||||||||||||||||||||||||||||||||||||||||||||||||||||||||||||||||||||||||||

Yarn 8
Eddie's Enterprise

Doc Thomas had been keeping an eye on Eddie and his camp followers; a bunch of hooligans if there ever was one, and he was puzzled by what he'd seen, and heard. There was a heap of scurrying around going on, but none of it made a lick of sense. The weaseling bunch had been seen gathering in strange places at strange times. One of the places was a huge warehouse that no one was certain belonged to anyone except a flock of really messy birds and rats; big rats! The place was just outside the city----or in this case, the town, limits. All this was announced by the private detective Doc had hired as soon as he heard of the strange shenanigans in and around the place that might in some way involve him and his enterprise; the selling of Alien Good Luck/Conversation pieces.

Now it warn't any business of Doc's except that he had no trust to spare when it came to the rascal, Eddie. The worrisome thing about it was, Doc figured Eddie couldn't be trusted even if he someday sprouted a set of angel wings, and was sporting a halo around his shaggy head.

A hair restoring treatment Eddie had cooked up and used on Doc had convinced him; for the fifteenth time, that the rascal Eddie couldn't be trusted. It shouldn't have happened Doc knew, but after a quart of pure white-lightning had been guzzled down, he had let Eddie use the poultice. It hadn't healed Doc of his falling hair at all. Instead, it pert-near took the entire scalp and most of the remaining hair off Doc's lop-sided pate. Them corn-cobs had been pure misery indeed!

The last time they'd come together Doc had overcome that varmint, and wound up with a good bank account. He'd finally got the best of Eddie and his crew of camp followers who seemed to worship him--------but dad-nab-it, *something* was brewing; anybody could see that.

Doc had his man out there, and he had reported a few dented, rusty trucks of all sizes hauling stuff into that old warehouse that once was used by the railroad; Doc could remember that far back. The trains were gone now---in that vicinity; the tracks had been hauled away for scrap.

Anyway, listening from cover of scraggly bushes the detective used his best recall talents and later told Doc everything he had learned or suspected. The scant ring of hair that was left on Doc's dome stood out like a riled-up porcupine, and the shivers and vibrations that raced over Doc's body were felt by Prowler, the spineless hound-dog that cringed somewhere beneath the house; Doc never had discovered exactly where that might be.

About all that was known of the dog was he had the constant shivers even when he slept, and that too was because of Eddie! Doc had found it necessary to provide Prowler with an entrance to a hidey-hole somewhere beneath the new house when they'd built it. At all hours during the night the hound could be heard mourning, moaning and groaning something fierce. All Doc could do was feel sorry for the dog, and curse at the very thought of the thirty-year old juvenile delinquent called Eddie who had ruined the bestest hound-dog ever born.

Now Doc decided to put his health, wealth and maybe his life on the line, and investigate the situation for himself; accompanied by the detective, of course.

Eddie had never stopped trying to figure out a way to top Doc's take-over of the 1939 Ford rod insert deal; it had hurt him for a time, but he had overcome. Doc would never have been able to take the scheme away from Eddie and his bunch if it hadn't been for Doc's nephew or some such; a kid by the name of Justin Case who they'd paroled from some upstate prison. The law had control of the guy again, but Doc was still free and likely always would be since he had no more mind than a hog that had got into some sour-mash and was drunker than a biled owl.

Well, what was past was past, and now Eddie was ready to set the world on its ear with a scheme that someone should've thought of fifty years earlier, but hadn't. But Eddie had, and just recent; about five months earlier in fact when it settled firmly into his mind what a preacher had told him years earlier. Five months ago it came back to him when he recalled a candy-bar vending machine and the huge amount of coins it gulped down and he himself had been a victim of the things at one time or another. About two percent of the time nothing came out, and being Americans and candy snappers to boot they'd take the loss and slap in another dollar or whatever the price happened to be. Eddie had been pondering the thing every few days since then, getting it set in his mind and now he thought he had it all figured out.

Once there were machines that sold most any article small enough to slide out the chute.

However of late, in the past few years, things had been changing; the machines were being recalled. Why? Probably something politicians cooked up for some crazy reason!

Whatever the case, it seemed the owners of businesses had started putting the products inside, on shelves, seeing to the sale of the wares themselves. There were fewer and fewer machines that sold cigarettes, candy, chips, and such; the machines were winding up in junk yards! Of course the ones where a person could rent videos had taken over, but Eddie decided that wouldn't last long. It seemed all good things were going the way of the old time drive-in movies.

And yet, Eddie and his bunch *had* made a goodly amount from the last deal they had sponsored before it fizzled out, and they used it to good advantage. They still had a slow but steady flow of cash coming in, and they used that to rent a portion of the old railroad right-of-way that included the ancient brick and metal building. They had rigged up an extra heavy log-chain they'd snitched from some nearby farm, a chain that protected farm equipment from being hauled off. Now it would provide a barrier to protect a new business.

The original owners of the vending machines found the devices little more than sheet metal, not worth repairing so they were piled near the city dump. The gang of hoodlums sneaked them away by night, spray-painted them front and sides and chained them near the front of the old warehouse. Chalk Meyers came up with enough empty packs; just packs for show, to fill the display windows. Someone had scrounged up a pop machine; that was the heaviest one of the lot, many of those were still being used and this one supposedly dispensed any of six drinks. It was a God-send for them.

The day came when Billy Bob, asked how the things would work with no innards?

"Well, B.B, how much does a pack of cigarettes set you back?"

"Gee, I don't know----somewhere around five bucks I reckon. Heck---who can smoke? When I do smoke it's just ground up leaves---can't hardly afford a plug these days.

"Right! But what if we sell a pack of cigarettes for a buck?"

"We buy them at five dollars, and sell them for one? It ain't gonna work, Eddie. We'd go broke right off the bat."

"Yeah, we would if we retailed them like folks expect, but we ain't going to do that."

"Eddie, if a man pays for something, cigarettes or a candy bar, he'll want a pack or a bar!"

"You're right." Eddie said. "They will expect to, but they won't get it. A few years ago a preacher told me he had studied human nature, especially Americans, and he said he'd discovered most citizens had a propensity-----whatever that means; for dropping coins into slots, and I'm betting he was right. Some will get riled aplenty---sure enough, but a big bunch of them will just dig into his pockets for more coins."

"NO!"

"Oh, yeah. That's what these signs are for----lookit, see? Ever one of them is the same, and a mighty good job they are."

"But Eddie-----that's awful! It's a hurtful thing. Maybe someone what don't know no better will drop his quarters in for nothing."

"Well, then I reckon they ortta learn better. The signs don't promise them a thing. Here's some tape, let's get them all fastened on good and tight."

There was usually a crowd of folks passing by, and they couldn't miss the bright banners flying above the vending machines, but what really drew a crowd were the signs. They pulled the crowds in. For a month or so Eddie or one of the others was busy rolling quarters and stacking them like miniature cord-wood. To make it more successful there was some kind of festival going on during the second and third week after the opening and the crowd passing was packed coming and going. Eddie and his gang had seen the impossible happen; after each encounter with the vending machines, first one then another would dig into pockets or purse and try the same slot, or move on to another only to have the same results. Eddie silently thanked the preacher of years past for such a brilliant idea. He and all the rest of his gang knew it couldn't last though. The police had been by several times a day right along, and they were sure to find something illegal about the operation before long. All they knew about it now was Eddie had a right to be there, and he had been wise enough to get a permit for open air sales operations. For the time being it seemed everything was going fine.

And that was why Doc, along about the fifth week of the odd goings on, penned his dogs and openly visited Eddie's place of business.

The problem was—there were no parking places, and it was maddening the way he had to creep along while he waited for the crowd to part enough so he could drive through.

He was worried one of the crowd, most of them youngsters, would dent or scratch his new Lincoln. He'd only had it for six months and he'd tried to take good care of it.

There wasn't much he could do about the interior. It was pretty well chewed up by his dogs, but he felt he should take them out every couple of days----out to the park where they could do their business. Sometimes one or more didn't quite make it, but Doc had a big spray bottle of Lysol, and he had been pricing seat covers.

Now he gave up and returned home, fed the dogs, and got ready to turn in. Somewhere beneath the floor Prowler turned onto his back and scratched the floor. Doc reached for the rake beside the bed; pulled a few more splinters from the floor, and the dog settled down. It left Doc thinking a new carpet and floor should last longer than half a year. Why in blazes couldn't Prowler move into the new addition with the other hounds? It made no sense at all!

Next day he hit the road at early evening, driving slowly, and got a good look at Eddie's enterprise. After a few blocks, he turned around, got on the north side of the street and crawled to a stop no more than thirty feet from the display. Eddie recognized Doc's car and trotted over.

"Hey there, you ol' fogey; how ya doing?"

"Stay back , you derned weasel! Don't you come no closer!"

"Well, hey—Doc? I'm just so pleased to see you; been planning to look you up---cut you in on my money-maker---it's a real gold mine." Eddie pulled out a roll of bills; he'd found it a real chore to carry the quarters around. Doc's eyes got big as silver dollars and kind of watery like he was scared enough or hurt enough to bust out in heavy tears any second.

"Yesterday's take," Eddie said. "For a thousand bucks you could get in."

"Yeah? A thousand?"

"You'd get a quarter for your part; count on it."

"Well, I don't know---you ain't been too good to me, and you done ruint ol' Prowler."

"A thousand dollars Doc, and you're in for a quarter!"

"You said that before."

"And I mean it sure as spit is wet---you'd be in for a quarter."

Doc scratched his head for a minute; the thing with the smashed car parts was winding down, wasn't going to last much longer, and when the cash from that was gone, how'd he feed his dogs? He was beginning to see renewed dollar signs floating before his eyes. He left Eddie standing there with a grin on his face, and thirty minutes later he handed over a thousand dollars. Eddie wrote out a receipt for a quarter, and Doc stuffed it into his pocket without a glance at the writing on it. Greed! The crowd was thinning out now; whatever had been going on at the park up the street or at the fair-grounds just beyond, must be about over.

Eddie was cutting it close. Chalk Meyers and B.B. Barton were already coming down the street. The other guys were inside the old building all set to help load the machines onto the already junked trucks. It would be a close thing, but Eddie figured they'd make it before the law checked the premises again.

Just last evening the police had stopped a fight before it got ugly; right within kicking distance of the vending machines, and the police told Eddie they thought he should take his operation somewhere else.

"But officer, am I doing something unlawful? Cause if I am, I'll make it up to the town."

"Nothing illegal as far as can be determined; just almighty strange."

"Yeah, I know-----but you may be right," Eddie had replied. "We'll move tomorrow night after the crowd dies down."

And they kept their word; taking everything with them---including Doc's thousand dollars. They had used the back of one sign where Eddie had written so Doc couldn't miss it. It clearly stated Doc's name; "FOR DOC---HERE'S YOUR QUARTER AS PROMISED!"

A strip of clear tape held a single quarter near the center of the sign!

"Dad blast it! A skinny quarter---I get a quarter, and they get my thousand! RATS!"

As he slid into his car the sign settled onto his lap, and he saw the reverse side. Eddie had planned it well; the proof was right there; it lay in his lap. Them rats had seen the same thing; they all knew that Doc would be in a rage when he discovered he was left all by his lonesome. He jammed the Lincoln into drive; wadding the sign that had swindled so many, including himself, of good money. He wiped his brow as he drove off, the one remaining sign crushed on his lap. It was identical to all the others Eddie had pasted up! It proclaimed the truth and was a bald-faced lie.

Doc shuddered as he read the words again! THESE MACHINES ARE HERE FOR ONLY ONE PURPOSE. THEY ARE TO DROP YOUR QUARTERS INTO----THERE WILL BE NO PRODUCTS FORTHCOMING---NOTHING AT ALL! ALL PRICES ARE A MERE FOUR QUARTERS. GOOD LUCK AND BE HAPPY!

It had Doc shivering and so mad he could barely think; and even his thoughts had stutters:

"O—oh i-if if only I h-h-had J-j-justin Case b-b-b-b-back, the two of us would s-s-s-show them ch-i-ises-s-l-l-ling we-we-we—weasels."

Doc could barely see through the tears of frustration, and humiliation. He thought he might go home and join Prowler in the hidey-hole he had dug out somewhere beneath the house.

Yarn 9
Eddie's Good Deed

Next evening Doc dragged Prowler from beneath the house and stuffed him into the passenger seat of the old S-10 pick-up. It had been rough; almost too much for Doc, but he had figured the activity would help ease the stiffness he'd been having in his feet of late, an aching, throbbing, pin cushiony kind of thing.

At least twenty other coon-hounds piled into the back so that the rear tires near flattened out. It was an odd-looking cargo as Doc headed for the thick woods just north of Kurtzville. The dog beside Doc was wild-eyed---whimpering; staring at the crazy man who actually had a hold of a wheel---such a dangerous thing to do! It made his neck hurt, and brought faint memories of the last time he'd chased a car---those awful wheeled contraptions!

Anyway, that's how it started. But walking through the woods in the dead of night, a wall of hounds on every side only made Doc's feet throb to a greater extent. That's when, despite the fact he should have known better, he decided to go home and tell Eddie, the town rascal about it, and the next day he faced the scamp.

"Just because I'm telling you about it Eddie; don't mean I want you to heal me. You've healed me until I'm nearly healed to death! I've gotta do something because I'm about a year behind on my sleep not to mention my dreams. I thought maybe you would know somebody who could help me. I'm telling you---life is killing me, and these feet are helping it happen."

"Well, Sir---I'll tell you what. Let me see if'n I can contact a Podiatrist and get you some relief. Maybe use some pills or a topical balm like they rub a horse's legs with. "

"Get me some relief? You're starting to sound like one of them! This Poddy thing---is that some kind of doctor? You know how I feel about them----don't trust them at all! No siree!"

"A Podiatrist is a foot doctor, Doc. They can't do you much harm by feeling of your feet."

"And I'm supposed to believe he'll stop with my feet? Every half inch higher he gets means another fifty dollars or more. You know that! Man, you've got more faith than I've got!"

"Now come on, Old fellow. If'n you don't want me to heal you, at least let me find someone else who is trained in that sort of thing. There's bound to be one or two in our town."

"Well---okay, but you make sure he don't be foolin' around where he's got no right to!"

"Done. I'll get right on it and you'll know the why, where, and what for by tomorrow."

Eddie left and before the day was out, he had made an appointment three days hence, just after noon. He let Doc know about it and the man got all shaky; said he'd be ready, but after the hike through the woods, he'd probably need a driver.

"These old feet might not be able to work the brakes," he complained, kicking at one of the twenty or so hounds that stood wagging their tails in a questioning way.

"Don't worry about that—I'll drive you personal," Eddie told him.

"Fine, amen, much obliged." He took a shuttering look around, then; "I'm getting old, man!" It kinda wheezed off into a pity-party whine.

"Well, Doc---don't you reckon getting old is better than not getting old?"

"What do you mean by that?" Doc asked, squinting one eye like Festus on Gunsmoke.

"I mean, Doc, if'n you stopped getting older then you'd probably be dead, don't you see?"

"Yeah---there is that. How does it feels to be dead, you reckon?"

"I ain't planning on finding out just yet. Listen, you be sure to scrub your feet plumb up to your ankles. You don't want the doctor thinking you're some homeless tramp," Eddie told him.

Doc was startled!

"You think he'll check that far up?"

"Oh, yeah, you bet. Now you take it easy; I'll see you day after tomorrow---long about noon."

Doc had been waiting, and at the sound of Eddie's horn on the scheduled day he hobbled from the house, across the porch, and down the two steps to the ground; sorta kicking dogs out of his path. He limped toward the old '56 Ford truck that folks accused Eddie of driving off the Ark when Noah wasn't looking. The thing still ran like a top, and after the S-10 the Ford, seemed to Doc to ride like a limousine. He settled back, relaxing for the ten block drive. Eddie parked in the nearest vacant space and helped the jittery patient inside.

"Good grief---all I see are women," Doc said in a loud whisper.

"Shhh! Bookkeepers and the like---a receptionist over there; she'll see you to the doctor. Are your feet clean?"

"Yeah---half way to my knees, an---"

"Mr. Thomas?" It was the receptionist---holding a door open. Eddie helped Doc to his feet, advising the woman he'd be going in with the patient. She nodded and led them to an examining room where she removed the man's shoes and socks. He sat on the examining table and fidgeted for a few minutes; reluctant to recline, and then the door opened, and another woman walked in. A woman!

Doc got bug-eyed and was soon near hyperventilation, and when the Doctor focused on her patient he began to sway and threatened to roll from his perch. Eddie reached out and steadied him; putting him on his back, pulling him up until his feet rested well on the table.

For a moment there was silence, then the Podiatrist took a bare foot in each hand; studying them intently---saying nothing for a time, but then!

"Tell me, Mr. Thomas—how long ago did you have your appendectomy?"

Doc went hyper, all wall-eyed---jolted as though he'd been hit with a thousand volts of juice. His upper body snapped and turned him into an L; frozen there---stiff as a board---paralyzed; not a tremor. He existed in that position for a long moment---unable to speak; then.

"Lawdy Mercy, Eddie! You done brung me to a witch doctor! Get me outter here!"

Between the Podiatrist and Eddie, Doc was calmed somewhat, and Eddie was pushed aside as a nurse took over. Doc wasn't sure he liked the idea of losing contact with the younger man even after all the many pranks the rascal had played on him over the years, but the nurse was a lot stronger than she looked; she held an ankle in each hand. Doc made himself a promise; if'n they tried to remove his breeches, he was leaving---shoes or no shoes! He flinched a bit when the Doctor let her fingers drift plumb up to his ankle bone; *horny woman!* How dare she do that? If'n that nurse, as strong as she was, tried that---well! 'Oh, Land a Goshen!'

"They've rolled my pants clear to my knees! I done told you, Eddie; I warned you!" Doc bellowed like he was having a panic attack.

The nurse, now looking around the room asked if anyone else smelled dogs; why did the place smell like a kennel?

Ready to bolt, she was.

"I'm allergic to dogs---especially hounds----I think I'm breaking out in hives! I'm going to be sick; I just know it---I'm---------." She headed for the door, hand over her mouth—eyes wild.

The Doctor continued to inspect the man's feet and without batting her eyes, stated:

"I see your ancestors were of the Welsh, Mr. Thomas. Were you born in Ameri----?"

"AAAHHHH! Great Caesar's Ghost!" Doc was sitting up again; ready to run; frantic—reaching out to Eddie.

"Don't be perturbed, Mr. Thomas. I was only referring to what I noticed in the alignment of your toes. You see how the ends of your toes sort of step down; with a straight-edge I could come very close to your ancestry."

"Oh, Land a Goshen! How can such a thing be? I gotta see a preacher, a priest, a NUN!" Doc was staring at his toes as if he'd never known they were there. He finally managed to continue.

"Oh, well, o.k., but I didn't like the idea of you trying to remove my pants from the bottom up! Taint natural and there could come a point when it'd get hurtful! Fact is, I know it would."

"I see." the Doctor told him, "I'll roll the pant legs down again; I can see why you're in pain. I want to fit you with some simple braces to help you walk in an ordinary manner, and without so much pain. I'll advise a few vitamins, minerals, and herbs which can be purchased over the counter. They will be a great help---I'll write a prescription for you to help restore the cartilage that has become badly eroded. My assistant will fit you with special inserts which you can change whenever you change your footwear, alright? The braces will be worn over your shoes, the inserts will go inside. You'll be shown how snug to lace the braces and all. Okay?"

Doc nodded---' How stupid did the woman take him to be, anyhow? Inside! Outside! GEE?'

But she was already gone, just like that.

Twenty minutes later the assistant came in with all the gear. When everything was in place, Doc simply could not believe it; his feet were feeling fine already. They felt beautiful and everlasting. Doc was glad to pay the bill even though it seemed to be astronomical. His feet made him want to walk off into the air and he silently thanked the podiatrist even if she was a horny, flighty woman---so ugly one had to call her beautiful because of her skill, and who could think of a word below ugly? She probably owned a chain of massage parlors where all manner of debauchery went on.

Doc wondered if she was married; he thought about asking her out----someday.

Eddie had stood near during the whole process, speechless. He figured he must be slipping to a fatal degree. Things like that couldn't happen! What would his followers think? What would they say? This was the first time in years he had failed to turn a decent act into a prank.

It turned out fairly well, though. All the boys recovered from the shock of Eddie's failure, they knew Eddie would be hitting on all eight cylinders within a week; two at the most. After all, that was the Eddie everyone knew, or knew about; the one everybody loved or feared---hated, even! That was----well-----that was-----Eddie!

Yarn 10
Doc's Dentures

Eddie felt like a failure; he was still tossing and turning at midnight that night, and with the dawn he felt worn out and useless. He struggled through the week until Doc came to his rescue several days later.

Doc Thomas had a problem, and he was hesitant about telling anyone about it. Even his hounds were forbidden to enter the house during meals because Doc thought they looked at him in a strange way whenever he sat down to eat. He knew how he must look and sound, what with his dentures flopping around like a flat tire on a car doing eighty; and then too, it was a hurtful thing.

Even Prowler, the hound Eddie the Rascal had healed of car chasing, had dared to creep from his hole beneath the house---seemingly concerned about his master's problem; *shrinking gums*. Doc had once caught the hound reared up outside the dining room window, looking in. Doc had been infuriated, but figured the hound had finally realized what the burlap bag behind the hubcap meant: "Don't chase cars!"

But that's a way back story; part of the first tale anyone ever wrote about Eddie. Doc had forgiven the hound, but even so he put shades over every window in the house. He didn't want any of his dogs to see him with his dentures flopping like a fish trying to walk.

It had been about three years since the healing of Prowler and there'd been a host of strange happenings between Eddie and Doc ever since. Every one of the capers would have been named a classic by the theater crowd, and no one could imagine a time when Doc and Eddie would sign yet another deal---- that would be unthinkable.

And yet, that's exactly what happened a couple days after Eddie got the word of Doc's miseries. He knew Doc Thomas had a thing about doctors and that he had a shivering terror complete with wild rambling eyes and hiccups at the thought of dentists. Even in a down-pour he'd walk around a block to get to his goal if there happened to be practicing dentist along the way and that had little to do with the outrageous fees the tooth Doctors charged. That was the reason he hesitantly contacted Eddie---thinking there might be a chance of that rascal helping. He told Eddie, quite candidly, that he had no intentions of throwing his money into the coffers of a man who spent his life prying teeth out of a person's mouth.

"But Doc, you ain't had real teeth for several years! What's the hurt of letting the man tighten up what they replaced them teeth with?"

"Well, the worstest part I reckon is the smell in them places, and the prices that are high enough to bankrupture a body. For the first time, thanks to that Alien Good Luck Charm/ Conversation Piece, I've got a savings and checking account that allows me to feed my dogs."

"Your hounds run the neighborhood, Doc. It's a marvel the city ain't stopped the trash and garbage run and closed the city dump. You got enough hounds to take care of all the trash around here."

Doc just shrugged; the only response possible because as he began forming an answer his uppers let go and clackity-clacked near past recovery.

After that Eddie hit the books---so to speak. He didn't have to do much research to find out all he needed to know in dealing with Doc; only the composition of the material used in dentures. Even so he kept Doc hanging on for another week; ignoring frantic calls from the man. Eddie had an uncle who was a dentist, and that's where he got the biggest portion of his info. Eddie knew exactly how to reline Doc's dentures; not a problem at all. Now when the originals were formed; that's the time a lot of study and practice had been needed, but finally he told Doc he was ready, and Doc asked if Eddie could maybe reline an earlier set since they were porcelain, and had looked like the real thing. They just didn't make things like they used to.

"I might Doc, but whichever one I do, I'll have to charge, impressions, you know."

"I ain't a'caring 'bout that---I got the money like I said, but I don't figure on bestowing it on no dentist. I'd gum a tough steak for a week before I paid one of them a red cent!"

"Well, I guess I could do this one thing for you---I'll get the fixings together. No telling what the stuff will cost, and I need some extra money 'cause one of my guys is in trouble."

"What? What happened? His teeth going, are they?"

"No---he's in jail, and a bunch of us are lucky we ain't in there with him."

"But—but—clack, clack but, but, they never goth you "cept that one time---no matter how many dastardly tricks you played----mostly on me, I must shay."

"That's because you were always there; like a target, you know, and really it was all in fun. This thing with Chalk Meyers---well, we were all into it, but only Chalk got caught. We was just funning; wasn't doing it for money. We'd bought us sun-glasses, and got hair dryers from a Good-Will store, shined our cars and parked in places like the police do, you know---half-way hide-a-way shelters. Chalk hair-dried/radared the wrong person—a real cop, and the cops don't think it's funny at all. Five hundred dollars will pay his bail. Can you do that?"

"Oh, sure. Money ain't a problem—when can you st-flubb-clack start?"

"Fetch me that porcelain set, and I'll get right on it. A week and you'll be gnawing corn off the cob; you can count on that."

Eddie didn't even bother his uncle---other than for a short phone-call—answered by the nurse who Eddie had dated several times---a sweet thing, she was too. From her he found out how the stuff should be mixed, and all the other things involved. But there was one other item; Eddie was a born rascal who couldn't resist making slight improvements on any job he took. He made some of those on the dentures, a couple of them, in fact.

His uncle, the dentist, would have had a fit if he'd known what was taking place, but he didn't know; only his assistant, the nurse, knew, and she directed Eddie in the operation being she was as much a prankster as Eddie. The two of them worked for hours on the uppers; worked until they had the reeds of a harmonica hidden in the lining process---

one reed on either side. The reeds were just a shade different in size, and thin as paper. The nurse, 'I don't dare mention her name,' she said making the reeds in that manner would set up an off-key harmonic vibration that could sound like a turkey gobbler, or the bugling call of a rutting bull elk. That information brought a sweat to Eddie's fore-head, and he had to ask the nurse how she knew such a thing. She just shrugged, and Eddie shivered.

Tiny holes led to the reeds that would rest between the old plate and the relining; a brain surgeon could have done no better; the air would exhaust— one stream on each side, between the upper teeth.

When all was in order, Eddie contacted Doc, and things went like clockwork; Eddie holding Doc's head with a hard right hand; his left gripping the man's chin---not too hard, but firmly. The tiny holes had been filled with a dissolvable substance that would vanish in a few days; four days, Eddie figured. He wanted to have the whole crew on hand when that happened and that meant going Chalk Meyer's bail. Eddie did a bit of trimming and buffing on the dentures before he let Doc use the mirror. That was a sight to see; Doc grinned from ear to ear, and slapped Eddie and the others on their back---happy as a clam, he was.

Eddie and his rascals left soon afterward, but were back four days later. Doc was brave enough to appear in the open by then and even Prowler had been sort of rubbing against his master's leg; though he did creep back to his hidey-hole whilst looking back at Eddie when that bunch appeared. The hound figured there was something almighty strange about Eddie and his friends; they made his eyes hurt. They reminded him of wheels, and wheels were the baddest of bad things. The hound didn't remember why that was so, but he did know wheels caused a funny feeling in his neck and a sick feeling in his innards.

Doc came down the two steps; his smile bright as sunshine as he came, dentures almost too white. About thirty hounds waited on the front lawn; Prowler sort of sniffed the air from the crawl space opening, but didn't come forth. It was during the home-coming atmosphere of the visit that the tiny drill-holes lost their blockage and allowed a small amount of air to pass.

All of a sudden, the dogs went crazy; howling and carrying on. Some chased their tails; others stood on their hind legs and howled. Prowler bolted from his hidey-hole and durned near succeeded in his attempt at climbing a persimmon tree.

Doc started yelling at the dogs, not yet realizing what had happened, and that's when the reeds cut in full blast, leaving Doc on his knees—staring past praying hands; searching the sky for all he was worth. The end of time must have just been announced; what else could make a sound powerful enough to grind its way out and around in all directions? Eddie and his bunch were as shocked as Doc, and all of them sneaked away---streaked away; figuring this time----this time, maybe they had gone too far. Dad-burn---he knew he'd gone too far!

Yarn 11
Feuds and Haints

After a good long spell things began to settle down, and Eddie sat back in a sort of reflective mood; repentant, maybe. But that was a thing that couldn't last; it was against his nature. A rat is born to be a rat, not a kitten. A few months passed, and the rat called Eddie, and his adoptive litter got so fidgety they could hardly sit long enough to eat a burger.

Doc was not much better. He had been fretting and carping for more than three months and he was not certain what the trouble was. At first, he blamed it on his old Chevy S-10 pick-me-up that had gone off track and dropped from twenty-four miles per gallon to barely three and a half, but that seemed to have healed itself because lately it was up to nearly eighty-five mpg, an unheard of miracle that had Doc rejoicing.

And then one day Eddie became rejuvenated. It became clear to all who took the time to study on it for more than a second that Eddie had not been that laid-back at all. He and his crew had been as busy as beavers all along; refilling the tank of the S-10 every night for a week before siphoning the tank nearly dry for the next few nights. These cycles came and went. Doc never knew when to fill up because as sure as he did, the tank seemed to get rid of it in some crazy way. He started keeping track of the pump prices, and the miles he drove, and for a while it seemed to him there must be a connection there----that fell through. The S-10 could not read the pump prices----it just couldn't.

But if not, then why would it work both ways? First punishing him, and then gladdening his very soul? And yet, the little S-10 was slowly bankrupturing him. The next time gas prices hit rock bottom, by *jimminy*, he was going to fill several five gallon cans; yessir!

'Nawh! Wouldn't work worth a dime. Eddie and his bunch of gangsters would consider his place their own personal gas station.'

Doc had never considered Eddie and his followers might be the culprit; causing his truck act up in such a manner. That in itself was more than strange because Doc always blamed them for every wrong thing under the sun. Then, after a long stretch of sky-high mileage and other good happenings, Doc had pert-near forgotten there were real live rascals in the neighborhood who could almost turn the world up-side down. He had no reason to suspect they were adding to and siphoning from the fuel tank of the little truck. He hadn't seen hide or hair of them for a month or more. He did recall hearing they were busy pestering some poor soul in the next county.

Still, how could that be when one of them, Billy B. Barton was still around? He had been taking care of Doc---doing the chores, running errands in Doc's truck; stirring up some pretty good meals. There just warn't any reason to suspect the kid of causing the truck to do all them crazy things; messing with the gas mileage. It was enough to make a man throw up his gizzard, and that feeling, although it had eased up of late, was rough on any man.

Doc started watching Billy more closely. Could he be messing with the truck? Nah! Surely not; after all, the kid seemed to be a jewel lately. Doc had considered adopting him, but he wasn't sure the boy ever had parents----likely he was just---there! A little addle-headed, yeah, but not too bad; just a kid being a kid-----but dad nab it, how old does a kid get to be?

Things were still going down-hill in the strangest way; that was for certain. Doc was feeling jittery as a lightning-bug with its ignition system back-firing. He was distracted for a moment as Prowler scratched fleas or ticks in his hidey-hole under the house. Ever since Eddie had healed the hound of chasing cars the dog had been a nervous wreck. Doc had finally persuaded the Vet to put Prowler on Xanax, and he did. Doc had bawled like a baby when he saw what a change it made on the hound. The dog would actually stick his nose out of the crawl-space, although he did look a mite cross-eyed at times. Doc felt somewhat blessed; he actually smiled.

And then one day Eddie and his gang reappeared. Doc thought he was having a heart attack when he got the news. He gulped down a couple of the pills meant for Prowler, and was dizzy all that day. It seemed that Eddie had added a new man to his gang.

But then someone reported the guy was an artist, and the only artist Doc had heard about had hurt no one but himself when he cut off an ear; not much danger there! Of course this fellow might be snooping around looking to steal dogs---might be a good idea to enclose Prowler safely beneath the house during the night hours. Doc developed the tremors, but they went away after B.B. returned from town with news that he had seen the new man and he seemed the friendly sort. There was no way Doc could know the whole gang had been there the night before; getting a feel of the place; showing the new man around----siphoning a little gas and such. Chalk Meyers stopped in to visit B. B., and Doc discovered the new man---the artist, went by the name, Dewey Stanky. Doc had to pinch himself to keep from laughing, but a sharp snicker got through.

It seemed Eddie and Stanky had become friends. Eddie admired the guy even though his parents must have been crazy; the last name---well, not much could be done there, but-------heck, early on the Dewey had become Dew, and so it had remained until someone thought to add an initial---an' A.' Everyone could tell when Dew A. Stanky was around---they made jokes about it.

But anyway Dewey seemed to fit right in, and the afternoon passed in a tolerable manner. Doc had surprised himself by actually shaking hands with the artist. In time they went their way and only Doc and B. B. were left. Doc was plagued with thoughts of ghosts because Mr. Stanky had brought the subject up during the idle talk and with night coming on Doc grew more and more jittery. Stanky had wanted to meet with Doc again and interview him in greater depth, but Doc had said he'd think about it; now the older man was having second thoughts. After all, the talk was concerned with a long ago feud and scary threats. Still, maybe the interview would be alright as long as Stanky didn't do or say something that would rile the ghosts so as they'd float around under the house and put a hex on Prowler. A couple of days passed while Eddie drove Stanky around, buying this and that. He began regretting hiring the artist since the fellow was burning through money like it was sawdust.

Eddie understood the artist would be doing a lot of unusual work; but some of this stuff? He wanted a quart of activated charcoal, thumb tacks, paint----big sheets of cardboard------for templates, he said, and box knives----all manner of do-dads! B.B. Barton was still acting as Doc's houseboy/chauffeur----his errand boy, and Doc was beginning to get used to it even though he couldn't understand how it came to be. He'd had a key made for the S-10 since B.B. seemed to be a safe driver. Doc was beginning to enjoy the good life. He had a bank account and a helper plus an S-10 that sometimes got close to a hundred and thirty miles per gallon!

***

A few days later Eddie and the gang showed up. Mr. Stanky rode with Eddie. They'd stowed all the fixings in Eddie's Ford truck; several large pieces of cardboard, paint, all the rest.

The artist was all fancied up and now carried a briefcase full of old documents---like some fancy official. They parked outside Doc's house; strutted up the walk and sat heavily on the porch swing. Stanky weighed more than two hundred pounds and when he dropped hard into the swing the porch threatened to disengage from the house. Doc took a chair opposite him, and the others gathered around.

Stanky opened his fancy briefcase that cost Eddie close to eight dollars at a Goodwill store. He withdrew several papers and forms that were tattered and torn; some appearing to be close to two hundred years old. They were yellowed with age. Doc was impressed; this Mr. Stanky must be as fine a man as ever came down the pike. Even B.B. sat up and took notice of how the man handled those ancient forms.Doc was feeling important; he wasn't sure why he felt that way, but there was something about a famous, suited up man being friendly right in your face. After a rather reflective moment Mr. Stanky looked up and got right to it.

"Now Mr. Thomas----er, Doc, I don't know what you may have heard about me---if anything, but some of your neighbors have mentioned battles that occurred around here ages ago. I've been on this case for years, much like my father before me. These battles---feuds actually, were bloody and involved several families. At one point the hostilities moved through this area."

"Lawd have mercy!" Doc belched the words out, his eyes as big as silver dollars. "When was all this?"

"Well, Sir, it was some-time around a hundred and fifty years ago. The thing is---well, as the last two were each choking the other to death----it's not known if either of them actually died there, but as they were in that position they avowed----'I'll see you in a hundred and fifty years, you lying skunk----ON SPOOK DAY!' Now Doc, I can't say for certain they even celebrated Halloween way back then, but I do know----from these forms that the time mentioned ends this month and is coming up pretty shortly. Have you had any odd experiences in the time you've lived here?"

"I've had so many that---well, I don't know where to start. About two years ago I had my upper lip as near as spit pulled right off my face. I had to stand lop-sided for over a month just to shave---uh, uh, would that count?"

"Indeed it might; at present there's no way to tell, but I'll make a note of it."

And so it went. Mr. Stanky and Eddie left to prepare for events further down the road.

When all were gone Doc turned to B.B., rather puzzled.

"I thought he was with y'all."

"Stanky? Naw, he's just been trailing along----- trying to get a hook on that feud thing."

"You think it's true?" Doc asked, his voice quavering.

"Oh sure. I've heard some really old timers tell ghost stories about it---terrible things, feuds!"

Next day Doc wanted to go over to Kurtzville to get some of the dog food he had stored there, and B.B. said he needed to make a last of the season's mowing of the lawn here, so Doc fired up the S-10 and drove off. B.B. made a few fast swipes at the lawn, thinking about all the lies he'd told in his life; most of them to pester Doc and others. Lying was a sin, folks said and B.B. agreed, but what was a fellow to do when there was nothing else to do to pass the time?

He had just put the mower away, and had a late snack when Eddie and the gang descended on the property. Stanky had several large sheets of cardboard and he began forming templates in various shapes; men on their back, curled up, spread-eagle; the guy was a whiz with a box-knife.

They moved Doc's bed and placed a form smack dab on the carpet just below where Doc would be sleeping. Stanky blew a puff of charcoal through a half inch pipe. He got the angle just right and when the template was removed the shape of a man was plain as day----just a thin shadow, but clearly in the shape of a man.

The bed was replaced; the bedding wrinkled in the manner of the sloppiest house-keeper, but Eddie declared it perfect. Another image was puffed onto the rumpled blankets and sheets, sort of like a dark frost, it was, but something that could not be missed. They were ready to move outside, but Eddie wanted a real, 'tear your scalp off,' kind of thing; just for fun.

Some of the guys tried to talk him out of it; said Doc was getting along in years---said maybe they should go easy on him for a while. Eddie said no; that Doc had tried to cheat all of them out of the big profits from them 39-Ford rod insert/ Alien Good Luck/ Conversation pieces, and he ought to pay the piper. One of the guys asked who the Piper was, but he got no answer as Eddie himself was not too certain who that might be.

Eddie had Stanky put one of the forms on the ceiling directly above the bed. Two of the guys stood on the bed and maneuvered a template into place and Stanky puffed a mist of something onto the space and followed that with a whisper of the charcoal. One couldn't notice the thing unless they were directly below, and that's where they expected Doc to be one second before, he spotted the shape.

They all left to puff signs here and there across the mole-infested lawn. They edged one on the driveway in a manner that would not be easily noticed; all the more threatening---and scary! One was leaning in a lazy way by the entryway to Prowler's abode. As Mr. Stanky was applying it the hound began moaning and carrying on something fierce, and the form was left there with only one leg.

By the time Doc returned home, plumb pooped out and ready for bed, all of the boys had found hiding places. They waited for Doc to emerge from the bath room; clad in some awful-looking sleep-wear, and even as he fell toward the bed, he noticed the form and screamed. B.B. came running; Doc was as white as a sheet. B.B. grabbed the bedding and shook it out. Doc doubted he'd sleep that night, but the boy calmed him down a bit.

"Come on, Doc; I'll fetch fresh bedding."

And he did so. Pillows were fluffed, and Doc crawled onto the bed, somewhat relaxed, but the second he rolled onto his back one would have thought the bed was a trampoline. There was another ghost sleeping on the ceiling! Doc came within inches of the thing---screaming and clawing at the air.

Always one to help, B.B. offered to move the bed, but when the image beneath it became visible Doc started screaming for help from above.

"Oh, Lawdy—Lawdy, shine your light on this 'ol sinner------Shine your light on me!"

"Lord have mercy---B.B., get that Mr. Dew A. Stinky over here right now! I'm getting a flash light and checking on Prowler."

He found a light and ran outside, along the house to the crawl-space opening. In seconds he spotted the faint, sooty outline; it was too much!

The hound was now threatening to tear the house off its foundation, and Doc was tearing at what was left of the hair on his pate. With eyes as big as saucers he ran this way and that, all over the lawn; stepping smack-dab in the center of another form--- this one with a reddish glow. It was as if that glow propelled him to near tree-top level and he plopped down close to another form, rolled over, and passed out.

Eddie sent Chalk into town to buy three of the biggest, best pizzas they had. He figured they may have over-played things a bit this time, but he usually felt that way. It was close to midnight when they put Doc to bed, swimming in beer and stuffed with pizza. His heart was glad and beating like the wings of a humming bird, but it was keeping him alive.

Yarn 12
Eddie's Change of Heart

By late morning the whole she-bang had floated out of Doc's mind and he began life anew. A couple of months passed, then a few more. The spring rains had begun and along with the moles Doc's lawn had been virtually destroyed. Adding to that, the hounds were always digging for the varmints until the house appeared to be built in a mud hole that would swallow the structure before the week was out.

Doc had taken to driving more often, and the mileage for the old Chevy S-10 was first up, then down. Once he had driven to his house at Kurtzville and on the way back, had run out of gas------this after Doc had filled it up the night before; he was certain of that. The receipt was still pasted on the dashboard, thirty two dollars and nineteen cents.

He knew a full tank should take him more than eighteen miles; he had known another thing also. Something had to be wrong. If he remembered correctly the fuel tank held around fifteen gallons; heck, an army tank, one that he knew about from way back, used about two gallons per mile! By Jove, here he was closing in on an old M-47 or some such.

He had walked to the nearest house and bought a gallon of fuel, hoping that---by some miracle, it would take him to a service station a mile or so further on. The little truck achieved that easily enough; Doc felt like kissing it right smack-dab on the radiator. He did just that before he walked onto the mud-coated lawn. He stopped by the areaway and spoke to Prowler, and heard an uncertain whimper. He threw a huge burger beneath the house. The dog barked a puppy-sized thank you, and Doc felt a love for the dog; one akin to the one he'd felt for the Podiatrist witch woman Eddie had taken him to; the one who liked to feel of his feet.

The next day was bright and sunny----and muddy; oh, yeah. And there were signs that the feudal ghosts were back. These signs didn't look like the ones before, but anyone could see their sign. Dad-nab it---they had walked all over the house with their muddy boots. One could see where they'd walked straight up the siding, then around the building---left—right, left---right, and below that were the tracks of another, and below that---still another one!

"LAWD----LAWD, how can such a thing be?" Still, spirits like ghost--just like witches and other haints, they seemed able to do things like these did last night! Great Scott---what would Eddie and his gang do? What would he do-----what could he do? As far as Doc knew no one had been able to defeat the haints in the talking piano, and some said the thing; or one like it had rolled all over the owner and squished him into mush. Doc wondered why he had never thought to get Eddie's phone number. As much as he distrusted and hated the weevil, still there'd been times when the fellow slipped and did a good deed. He called a neighbor kid who was willing to look Eddie up and tell him to come running; that the haints were back!

Eddie and several of his followers had gathered in the rear of the general store, expecting that Doc would send for help before the noon hour, and all because him and his crew had used muddy moccasins on long poles the night before and tracked around Doc's house; all the way up to the eaves. No way could Doc miss them! He had probably ground his dentures to dust over it.

Eddie had become repentant in the past few hours, and his cadre was at a loss as to what to do about it. They were bewildered and became even more so when Eddie joined them later on.

"Guys, did you ever wonder what it would feel like to do only good deeds for others and leave them wondering who did it? I mean----well, it's the same kind of thing, only we always leave them puzzled and scratching their heads like before."

"What kind of stuff would we do? What could we do?" Pete Simpson asked, agape; puzzled!

"Maybe we could heal his hound, Prowler," Eddie suggested. "Doc loves that old flea-bag."

"You done healed him until he won't come out if the sun is shining; he's afraid he'll see his shadow." B.B. put in.

"But could we survive if we did good for people?" Eddie asked. "Would we find that it's fun to play tricks on people, so it leaves them liking us even if they don't know who we are?"

"I believe that could be; yeah," Pete said. "And I think the best test ever is-----can we learn to do so in a way that'll let us live with ourselves. We don't want to end up like saints—you know what happened to a lot of them."

"One of us might have to sleep with a dog, and you know how a hound-dog smells; especially a wet one. If'n I go to heal Prowler it'll probably come to that; someone will have to make friends with that hound."

None of the guys could believe it when Eddie showed up in the rear of the grocery two days later. He had changed his brand of tobacco from Beechnut to a snuff that smelled strongly of something like

Wintergreen, and his lower lip had all it could hold; bulging out like some evil boil, but it wasn't enough; not powerful enough. The reek of wet hound-dog was so strong it could've covered the scent of a polecat that has its tail heisted.

All of the guys bummed a pinch of Eddie's snuff and every one of them, to kill the wet hound smell, tried it by the nasal route, and that brought on a sneezing revival that had all of them in a circle, patting the back of the guy in front. It did nothing to banish Eddie's odor from the premises, but the grocery owner figured it cleared up a lot of sinus problems as it killed the sense of smell of the partakers for a while. When the sneezing fits were over, Eddie told his group.

"I done it, fellows! It was no easy thing, but I'm here---vertical and ventilating but I feel I got through to the dark side of that hound even if it did cost me a couple of Big-Macs for him and a mess of stink for me. While I recuperate you guys are going to have to take over."

The gang was stunned. Charley Lowe almost swallowed his fresh chew. He recovered, and asked in a squeaky voice:

"If one of us has to go and make up with that hound, how do we keep from catching the same ventilating vinegar stuff that you've caught?"

"No, Charley---what I said meant I am standing tall and breathing normal like. I 'spectno germs are able to live around that dog so whoever goes will be safe. Say---I've got an idea! Let's put together a song for him------just a few lines 'cause he won't know what we're saying anyway. He won't remember it for more'n a minute. I seem to recall Charley; you play the Ukulele, right?"

"Yeah, Eddie---but it'd be tough playin' anything under there; no room."

"If'n you scrooch in on your back and kinda' craw-dad it along, I'll bet you can do it, and win ol' Prowler back to life. Doc would praise you no end!"

" But------but---b---." Charley stuttered to a stop.

"Atta boy; I knew you could do it. Now get started on that song---just a small ditty."

And so it went. Charley was always coming up with songs, some of them really good, others downright corny. This time it took him several hours, and that was only after he had gotten a good look at Prowler's hidey hole. He brought his Ukulele the next day and had a practice session before Eddie had time to get to the store. The guy who owned the store ran out before Charley could sing the ditty more'n once. He told three shoppers the place was closed because of a foul odor, and one of them allowed he knew what that odor might be.

Inside, Charley sung it again and all present thought the tune was pretty good, but the lyrics were extra corny. Charley went over it once more, his voice as twangy as a beginning yodeler.

"Prowler, chase your dreams—play real hard
Scoot your can---all over the yard,
Scratch the grass---then shake it off
Find a place---where the grass is soft.
Sleep for a time--- dig moles all night
But mostly remember ---to dig, dig life—**DIG LIFEeeeeee!**"

Eddie got there in time to hear the last four lines, and he had Charley do the whole thing over. He pronounced it as corny as corny could be, and then added.

"But I love it!"

Over the next few nights Doc Thomas dreamed of hearing faint sounds of an off key Uke, and a nasally voice, but it wasn't worth coming full awake for. After four nights of that, he let it drift into a sort of cacophonous drone, wind under loose shingles maybe or some such. Only once did he consider checking on Prowler, but the thought of the ghosts from the ancient feud put a stop to that!

Charley could take no more; Eddie would have to find another disciple; enough was too much, as Popeye would say.

And Prowler? Well, he was aroused the next couple of nights by Eddie who came near the crawl-space area and thumped on a two-stringed doodad he had put together while he sang the ditty extra low lest he rouse Doc. Of course Prowler had thoughts of his own concerning the music; it hurt his ears for one thing. After the first two nights of the caterwauling, Prowler got as close as possible and fixed the noise-maker with a hypnotizing stare until he found there was something in the noise that made a funny sensation plumb down his gullet, and he found himself whining in the craziest way. The dog had gotten in tune with the clamber-maker and by the end of the session the fourth night he was a changed animal. He found the sound soothing for some strange reason and he came out to welcome the demon that had pert-near wrung his neck about three years earlier. Somehow Prowler sensed a change in the rascal. The dog felt a change in himself also; one that left him baffled, but he couldn't help hoping a big wheel would come along and get every one of them trouble makers; even the one that made the terrible ear-hurting noise coming out of that little box that had strings on it.

He began digging for moles, getting most of them, and it seemed he had a constant urge to scoot his can all around the yard. It was a soothing thing. It eased the pain in his chewed on tail.

Doc Thomas got together with Eddie and told him of his own feelings.

"I don't understand how you did it, Eddie, but it looks like you've finally healed Prowler. And I got these fancy comfortable shoes and braces now; thanks to that horny Podiatrist and she has agreed to go Coon hunting with Prowler and me; what do you think of that?"

"Well, I'm plumb glad for you, Doc. I guess a person sometimes has to get near blind before he sees the light but, GEE WHIZ-----somehow it's----it's like the whole town is dead and dried up now; in mourning, ya know?"

"Yeah." Doc returned with a far-away look in his eye.

The gang was cutting cards back at the grocery; trying to pick their new leader! Some of the guys had tears in their eyes. History had been made and they had witnessed it---been a part of it! Yes, Sir---they had changed the world and somehow, by some miracle, the world had survived and changed them.

THE END

Author Joseph Sexton

After two years in the army, most of it in Korea in 1952/53, I bought a moving company and made good money in the transfer of furniture. I would work all day, then sing and play a big part of the night away. I knew several of the big stars but my idol, Hank Williams, had passed away while I was in the military, so I never got a chance to meet him, although I was backed up several times by some of his band. One night I was singing, "Blue Darling," when I saw my wife-to-be, and something said to me---She's The One, and she has been for almost 63 years.

I have written about 1500 songs, poems, recitations, etc. There's been 7 novels published along the way. For several years I was part of a jail ministry; first in the detention center, then the jail. Once I told the sheriff I wanted to go to the penitentiary, that I had all my paperwork and shots. He said NO! I told him that if Johnny Cash had been allowed to do so, I should too, but he wouldn't back down.

Things are pretty bad when one can't buy his way into the big house, but the sheriff was a good guy. In the spring of 2017 I had to give up the jail routine due to bad health. I have written an unknown number of short stories and always have several underway; some humorous, some that would scare the socks off you. Almost every part of the, "Truth About Eddie," series is true, factual---actually happened; I just pepped them up a bit.

Printed in June 2019
by Rotomail Italia S.p.A., Vignate (MI) - Italy